CW01619364

THE CRASH

ALSO BY TOM BESTWICK

When Karma Comes Calling

Black & Blue

Keep on Digging

THE CRASH

A 'WHEN KARMA COMES CALLING' STORY

TOM BESTWICK

Copyright © 2025 by Tom Bestwick

All rights reserved. No portion of this book may be reproduced, copied, distributed or adapted in any way, with the exception of certain activities permitted by applicable copyright laws, such as brief quotations in the context of a review or academic work. For permission to publish, distribute or otherwise reproduce this work, please contact the author at hello@tombestwickauthor.com.

ISBN (paperback) 978-1-0685606-2-0
ISBN (ebook) 978-1-0685606-3-7

Cover and book design by Christian Storm

To mum. For always helping me believe I could do anything.

"If you want to keep a secret,
you must also hide it
from yourself."

—**GEORGE ORWELL**

THE CRASH

1

The crunch of metal devouring metal.

Horns blaring.

Tires screeching.

Windows smashing.

A cloud of smoke.

The sickly blend of putrid fumes, burning rubber, and blood.

His own blood.

Or maybe other peoples' blood.

Incoherent shouting. Muffled, but still there.

Screams.

Like nothing he'd heard before.

A haunted melody.

Much closer this time.

Crying. Raw and urgent.

"Someone help me! Please!"

Sirens.

Out in the distance. Then much closer.

Fading vision, catching glimpses of frenetic legs.

Car doors requiring every ounce of strength to pull ajar.

Bodies being freed.

Bodies on the floor.

Bodies covered in blood.

Blood. So much blood.

Sombre hues of crimson pooling on the ground.

Compressions taking place.

Right before his very eyes.

He's going.

Going.

Gone.

[A LITTLE LATER. . .]

Jessica Johnson arrived home 30 minutes earlier, her head spinning with relief.

It was Tuesday. She'd stayed behind again to finish marking the last of her class's Key Stage 2 mock English papers — an agonising slog through misplaced apostrophes, tragic homophones, and punctuation so butchered it made her wince.

Like, come on, guys.

Jessica loved teaching, but this part of it was starting to grind her down. She'd been at Prendergast Vale School for a little over four years, working her way through the age groups after graduating from the Open University. But she had found herself contemplating just how much of a difference she was *actually* making with kids that were at an age where they didn't give much of a monkey about their education or future.

Not really, anyway.

Maybe secondary school would suit her better. At least those kids had started mapping their lives out — college, apprenticeships, work. Hell, they could launch a business with a few clicks if they wanted to. The possibilities were endless. Jessica believed, maybe naively, that the right teacher could change everything.

Ironically, Jessica hadn't had those options when she was a child. When she was their age, doors weren't just closed; they were bolted shut. Even the idea of opportunity felt like a cruel joke played on other people. Even getting a whiff of an opportunity felt like a part of life she wasn't allowed access to.

That was what drove her now — being the help she never had. Forcing those doors open so her students could walk through. Even if it took a fucking crowbar.

But maybe Jessica had been going about it all wrong. Originally, she'd wanted to be working with kids when they were young, inspiring them to love learning and strike a chord with someone who one day would go on to achieve big things — bigger things than what was expected of them — and cite her as being the reason why.

That, because she gave a shit when they were young, they were stirred to take on the world.

Again, perhaps she was being naïve. The truth was primary school kids are just going through the motions. They clocked in at nine, attended lessons and learned the basic shit, fooled around with their buddies, ate some crappy food, and clocked out again just after three when they toddled off back to mummy and daddy or some poor childminder

Maybe they did their homework. Or maybe they said their dog ate it.

Spoiler alert: either way, it doesn't matter.

Not really.

So maybe it was time for Jessica to start looking up the chain.

And with that thought festering, she'd kicked her heels off, poured herself a small wine, opened her Surface laptop and scrolled through to the TES jobs page. There was nothing around locally that was catching her eye.

The vast amount of jobs across the UK — there were over 500 — got her thinking of home.

And intrigue got the better of her. As it so often did.

She typed in the postcode of the orphanage she'd grown up in — it grates on her that she can still remember it despite trying to remove that stain from her life — and began to flick through the list of posts. There was one at an academy — St Andrews Academy. A class tutor position for the 2019/20 Year 7 group, mixed with English teaching duties.

It was almost too perfect.

But Jessica and her husband, Gregor, were settled in London. Their lives were here in Lewisham. She knew he would never want to give that up.

Yet that didn't stop her from bookmarking the tab and saving the job. She had a bit of time before the closing date.

As Jessica sipped her wine, she turned her attention elsewhere. She opened her Facebook and Instagram pages. The ones with a fake name, no friends, and no photos. It was there to serve a single purpose: to keep tabs on her two younger sisters.

She typed E into the search bar.

Sure enough, they both pop up at the top: Elizabeth and Esme. She clicked on Elizabeth's profile.

And like an ingrained routine, she'd begun to doom scroll through the posts, starting with the newest, finding out what she had been up to recently over the last few days, with her perfect family and perfect, cosy, life.

Then Jessica revisited the old posts and photos. Again.

The house was eerily quiet without Gregor and so she turned the TV on. Something — anything — to make the place feel alive.

Like she wasn't alone.

Up popped ITV news.

At first, Jessica wasn't paying attention.

But then she'd heard the reporter mention a crash on the M25 that had happened a short while ago.

Her head cocked up. It had her attention.

It wasn't just any old crash either. There was a breaking news banner that stated emergency services were responding to a major incident on the M25.

Well, that's Gregor not making it back any time soon.

That was her first thought. She was sure he was ok.

But she wanted to see how much it was going to hold him up.

Jessica pulled out her iPhone, thumbed across to Gregor's number, and hit call.

It rang out.

She cursed and tried again.

It rang out.

And that was how it continued until finally, she was called by an unknown number a few hours later.

TWO DAYS LATER

2

The first thing Gregor Johnson hears is a machine beeping.

He recognises the sound straight away. The sound drags him back nearly twenty years — back to the Nowy Szpital in Świebodzin, sitting at the bedside of his babcia (grandmother in Polish) as she recovered from a heart attack. The steady pulse of the monitor, the thick, cloying scent of disinfectant, the endless hours spent waiting for something — anything — to change.

He was a teenager then. Nearly 20 years had passed, but it had never left him.

He opens his eyes.

The world lurches into focus, but everything is off-kilter — colours too stark, edges too soft. A tight, sterile space bathed in natural light.

A TV hangs in the corner, screen black. To his right, a vase stuffed with purple chrysanthemums wedged between cards that wouldn't look out of place on a windowsill after a birthday. Left for a week or so. Then shoved in the recycling.

But these aren't birthday cards.

They're *Get Well Soon* cards.

Thinking of You cards.

What the hell happened?

Gregor tries to remember. It's all a blur. The last clear moment: locking his office door at Scale, the architecture firm he'd been with for a few years now. Laughing with Claire from HR as they crossed the car park. Joking about something banal. She was always good for a laugh.

Then climbing into his new Polo. The 18-plate he'd grafted for over a year.

Then thinking about home.

About the small glass of Sauvignon — because it was always Sauvignon — waiting for him.

And then...

Nothing.

Whatever happened between turning the key in the ignition and waking up here is lost in a void.

Gregor shifts, trying to move, trying to piece together where he is.

Something's wrong.

He can't.

It wasn't because Gregor was in too much pain.

It was that Gregor felt nothing at all.

"Will, 201 is waking."

Gregor's eyes flick to the door. That, at least, he could still do. One man and two women walk through into his room with a sense of urgency. All three decked in their unflattering baggy mint green uniforms so common in...

Hospitals.

The man — Will, presumably — moves to Gregor's left, his presence steady, authoritative. Gregor follows him with his eyes, then glances at the two nurses on his right. One black and the other, he assumes, is Filipina. Their faces unreadable.

But Will is the one speaking.

Gregor's throat tightens. His body feels wrong. Alien. He forces himself to speak, to keep his voice level.

"I can't feel anything," he says, trying to keep his voice composed. But it's useless. The words fracture, thin and ragged with panic.

His coolness — his control — leeches away as he tries, really tries, to move.

A twitch. A flicker. A single muscle contracting.

Nothing.

It's like those parts of him simply don't exist.

"Gregor, it's really important that you try to stay calm. Manila, can you—"

"Why can't I feel anything?"

Will keeps talking, passing orders to the nurse — Manila, apparently — without meeting Gregor's demand. Avoiding it. Holding something back.

Gregor's always hated that. People dodging the truth. Dancing around what needs to be said.

It tightens the panic in his chest like a fist.

"Will someone just tell me what the *fuck* happened?" The words come out with an explosion of spit.

"You're paralysed."

Silence drops over the room like a lead weight.

But that answer didn't come from one of the nurses.

Gregor knows the voice instantly.

The two nurses on Gregor's right part like a curtain, revealing his wife.

Jessica.

Standing at the entrance of his room.

Eyes puffy, skin pale, her usually pristine blonde hair limp and unwashed.

Looking as broken as he feels.

3

Gregor lies still, listening as Jessica tells him what the doctors won't.

There was an accident on the M25. A bad one.

A fatal fog had rolled in — thick, impenetrable — swallowing the road whole. It killed visibility first. Then, unhappy with that, it claimed four lives. The youngest, a six-year-old boy.

Many more were injured.

Many, many more.

Like Gregor, they'd all been brought here — to Spire London East Hospital. Some with minor injuries. Bruises, concussions, whiplash. Others with broken bones, shattered limbs, life-altering damage.

And then there was Gregor.

He'd tipped the scales completely.

He may never walk again.

He may never move his arms again.

He may never feel anything below his neck again.

Jessica, his wife of just over two years, kept talking, her voice steady, anchored. But Gregor had already drifted somewhere else.

Somewhere darker.

All he could think about was what he may never get to do again.

Designing blueprints for new office spaces, long drives out to the coast, swimming, playing 5-a-side, pouring a glass of red after a long day, walks around museums, shopping, sex. Gregor thought about the fact that he wouldn't even be able to take a shit without someone needing to wipe his ass for him.

The thought sent a fresh wave of nausea rolling through him.

Everything that had once been effortless was now an impossible hurdle.

Gregor turned his head away from Jessica, as much as his useless body would allow and asked her to let him rest.

"What? I'm going nowhere," she shot back, defiant.

A silence stretched between them before she spoke again, softer this time.

"Greg, look at me."

He clenched his eyes shut. Shook his head.

Pathetic. Like a fish flopping on dry land, gasping for something it would never get back.

"Look at me," Jessica demands.

This time, he did.

"I'm going nowhere."

That night, Gregor dreams.

He dreams of home — Świebodzin.

The elegant buildings and churches, the cobbled town square, the medieval walls. The air thick with the scent of fresh-out-the-oven pierogi and gołąbki. The sky burned orange, casting long shadows, illuminating the towering statue of Christ the King, arms outstretched over the town.

He dreams of Arek pulling up outside his house, honking the horn. Of kissing his mother, Ozella, quickly on the cheek before heading out to tear through the country roads. Of the crackling sound of old cassettes—Maria Awaria, Republika, Halina Frąckowiak — filling the car.

Gregor turns to face his pal. He's drinking a beer behind the wheel, singing in between hits of słodki nectar. Gregor takes a long swig of his own.

And then it's gone.

His eyes snap open.

The warm glow of Świebodzin is replaced by the dim, sterile light of the Spire London East Hospital ICU.

A trolley quietly rattles along. A nurse — a new face he hasn't seen yet — pops her head in.

"Oh, you're awake. Am I ok to do your obs? It'll not take long and I'll leave you at peace. Pinky promise."

Gregor nods. His voice, when it comes, sounds flat, detached. "Sure."

She moves to his left, setting up. He watches her work, already knowing what's coming. Another tiny drop of hope evaporates as she straps the blood pressure cuff around his arm.

Nothing.

No sensation. No pressure. Nada. Squat.

"Had a dream, did you?" She asks, glancing up.

Gregor blinks at her. Tight face, shoulder-length braids. A small nose stud catching the dim light.

"I went by earlier. You were mumbling in your sleep?"

"Ah, yes. I do that a lot, apparently."

"Well, I hope it was something sweet, at least."

"It was. I was dreaming of home."

"And where is that?"

"Świebodzin. Western Poland. About an hour outside of-"

"Poznań?" The nurse cuts in.

Gregor raises an eyebrow. He's used to people nodding politely, having no idea where he's talking about. Everyone's heard of Kraków and Warsaw. No one's heard of Świebodzin.

"You know it?"

"I know it. Me and a few friends travelled around Poland after finishing Uni a couple of years back. We took a detour while in Wroclaw and spent a night in Świebodzin before heading to Poznań."

"And what did you think?"

"Beautiful. Really beautiful."

A small, fleeting smile tugs at the corner of Gregor's mouth. "Yeah. It was a good place to grow up."

"I hope you don't mind me asking but the accent? It's not all that thick."

"English father."

"Explains the surname."

"It throws a lot off. You're not the first. Sorry, I didn't catch your name."

"Alexandra. Alexandra Calloway," she says, finishing up with the obs. She moves to the end of Gregor's bed and fills out the clipboard with the latest results. "But call me Alex."

"And how am I looking, Alex?"

"Obs, a lot better. Generally, you really want me to answer," she says with a sprinkle of daring sarcasm.

Gregor exhales a quiet laugh. "Yeah, I've been better."

"So," she says, clipping the chart back into place. "Let's not focus on that." A mischievous glint in her eye. "Tell me something different. What brought you to London, Gregor?"

For the next ten minutes or so, Gregor gives Alex a whistle-stop tour of the last decade.

Right back to 2008 when he moved to Lewisham to fulfil his dream of becoming an architect in the *greatest city on Earth*.

He'd come out of the Poznań University of Technology with a degree and belly full of ambition. But life rarely follows the plans you make in your head. He finds himself talking less about architecture and more about the woman who changed everything.

Before Jessica, his nights stretched into the early hours, his laptop screen the only glow in the room. A relentless grind to prove he was just as good — no, better — than his English colleagues.

Now, when he shut his laptop at the end of the day, he was hers.

Gregor hesitates. His mind drifts back to the M25, to how easily life can turn on a dime.

He swallows. "Is it possible..." He feels ridiculous asking, but he needs to. "For the feeling to come back?"

Alex doesn't answer right away. He can see it in her face — she's choosing her words carefully, weighing what to say and what to hold back.

"It's possible. Every case is unique, and it is entirely dependent on the severity of the damage to your cord. Looking at your notes, we should know more tomorrow."

Tomorrow.

Gregor stares at the ceiling. That single word settles like a weight in his chest. Well, it would if he could feel it.

Alex watches him. "Is there anything else I can do for you?"

"No. I'm good."

A lie, obviously. His face — at least that still works — probably betrays him.

Alex lingers a moment longer. Then, gently, she rests a hand on his arm.

Gregor feels nothing.

Absolutely nothing.

God, how he wishes he could. Just the ghost of a touch. Some small proof that his body still belonged to him.

"You've got the best people around you," Alex says, softly. "Try to stay positive, yeah?"

A cough from the doorway.

Not an accidental one — a pointed one.

Alex pulls away immediately as Jessica strolls over to the bed with a carrier bag and a packet of plastic straws.

"Not interrupting anything, am I?" she asks.

Gregor clocks the sharp edge in her tone.

"Not at all. I was just finishing off the obs," Alex says, sheepish. Like she's been caught with her fingers in the biscuit tin.

She steps back, professional again. "I'll leave you both to it."

DAY 3

4

Jessica felt the vibration of her phone before she even reached for it.

Knows full well who it will be.

Her fingers brushed the hard lip of her front jeans pocket, and sure enough, when she slid it out, the name flashed across the screen for the third time that morning.

Ozella Dąbrowska.

Gregor's beast of a mother.

Jessica had done the right thing. The obvious thing. She'd sent Ozella a text two days ago after the accident, letting her know Gregor was in hospital. Kept it brief. No fluff. Said she'd update her when there was something to say.

Apparently, that wasn't enough.

Because after 24 hours of very little updates and not hearing from her *Cenny Chłopiec* – Precious Boy – Ozella hadn't stopped badgering Jessica. Her iPhone buzzing like an incessant wasp around cider on a hot summer's day.

Why won't you answer?

What's going on?

When can I speak to Gregor?

But there was a reason Jessica was avoiding Ozella.

And it had nothing to do with not wanting to give updates.

Ozella was the kind of mother who believed nothing was ever good enough for her son.

And that included Jessica.

It had always been that way. From the very beginning. From the moment they met — at a funeral, no less. And not just any funeral.

Pola Dąbrowska's funeral.

Gregor's grandmother.

Jessica had flown to Poland with him, there to hold his hand as he said goodbye to the woman who had shaped his childhood. She'd heard so much about Pola. Tough as rusty nails. A straight talker. A fierce woman who took no shit. But a woman who was full of love. The kind of woman who held a family together.

You needed anything, you went to Pola. They don't make 'em like Pola anymore, she remembers someone saying.

"She'd have loved you," Gregor had said on the flight out of Gatwick.

Jessica had spent the journey listening to him reminisce.

Admittedly, Jessica had felt uneasy about going to the funeral. It wasn't lost on her that she would not only be meeting Gregor's mother for the first time on the most sombre of occasions, but *all* of Gregor's family for the first time on the most sombre of occasions.

But she'd swallowed that hesitancy. Sucked it right up and pushed it right down into the pit of her stomach. Smiled through it. Did what needed to be done.

Back to Ozella. Before they'd entered St. Michael's for the funeral, Gregor had introduced Jessica to as many of his family members as possible. Uncles, aunties, cousins, second cousins, nieces, nephews — A family the size of a herd. All clustered around in cliques. Each one, dressed in traditional heavy black. Each had given Jessica a hug, a soft kiss on the cheek. Said it was nice to meet her. Asked her how she was and said they were looking forward to getting to know her more while was staying with them.

All except Ozella.

She'd breezed past without so much as a glance. Wrapped Gregor in a tight hug, whispered something in Polish against his forehead. Held onto him like he was all she had left.

And then she was off.

This had not been the first time Jessica had been brushed off in her life. But this, this felt different.

"It's nothing personal," Gregor had assured her that night in his childhood bedroom. "She's just dealing with a lot."

But Jessica had known, even then, that it was personal.

Ozella had deep and traditional Polish roots and wanted the same for her son. In the whole time they'd been together, she'd persistently pleaded with Gregor to return to Poland and be with family. More so after Pola's passing. And each time Gregor said he was staying in London, Jessica knew Ozella laid the finger of blame firmly at her feet.

Jessica was the reason Gregor wouldn't come back.

The tension between them had never eased. Never softened. It had simmered beneath the surface for years. Until it finally reached its boiling point.

On her wedding day.

When Ozella had looked Jessica in the eye and asked the one question that ripped the air straight from her lungs.

"So, have you managed to convince Gregor to have kids yet?"

It was supposed to be the happiest day of Jessica's life.

They were back in Świebodzin. She and Gregor had married on a perfect late spring afternoon.

When she stepped out of the hotel that morning, the air had felt different. Lighter. Infused with the crisp, clean scent of blooming flowers and fresh foliage. As if the whole world had been designed just for her.

She'd bathed in the soft hues of lavender, pink, and golden yellow hanging from the trees, felt the warmth of the sun settle on her skin as it rose to bless her day.

Then came St. Michael's.

And they'd got married.

In front of the same people they'd seen at Pola's funeral.

Where there had been grief, there was now love.

Where there had been tears of loss, there were now tears of joy.

The sea of mourning black had been traded for Poland's finest and brightest elegance.

They had eaten. They had danced.

And it was when Jessica had taken herself outside for a moment's respite that she was joined by Ozella.

Even Ozella's niceties contained a layer of passive aggressiveness as thick as the vanilla buttercream that broke up the layers of her naked wedding cake.

And then she'd said it.

"So, have you managed to convince Gregor to have kids yet?"

The words had landed like a slap.

Jessica had always wanted children. Desperately. She wanted a family to raise, a life so different from the one she'd had growing up that it might as well belong to someone else.

But there had been a time when she thought that dream had been ripped away.

She'd previously had a miscarriage that had fucked her up so badly she wondered whether she'd recover.

And just when she thought she might never recover, Gregor had held her together.

With him, she had pictured a future where, one day, it would happen again. And this time, she would see it through to the end.

And yet.

Six hours into marriage, standing in the golden light of her wedding day, she learned the truth.

Gregor didn't want children.

Not now. Not ever.

It was off the table.

Ozella's question had triggered something — a chain reaction of resentment that only gained weight with time.

When Jessica and Gregor spoke about it, they inevitably argued. Ozella's question pushed right to the front of Jessica's brain and had remained there ever since.

Jessica knew Ozella was aware of the cavity she'd caused in their marriage.

A cavity that couldn't be filled.

And Jessica had never forgiven Ozella for that.

Before Gregor's accident, it had been over a year since Jessica had spoken a single word to Ozella.

What started as general dislike had hardened into something colder—mutual disdain. And that was fine. Jessica had long accepted that she would never win Gregor's mother over.

But now?

Now, the bitch wouldn't leave her alone.

As if she didn't already have enough on her plate, Ozella was becoming another problem. One Jessica had no patience for.

With a sigh, she stepped away from Room 201, searching for somewhere quiet. Away from prying ears.

Then, finally, she answered.

"Hey, Ozella."

"Finally." The woman on the other end exhaled sharply. "I've been trying to call."

"Sorry. Reception over here is patchy."

"Patchy. What is this? What do you mean?"

"Not so good."

"Ah. Understood." A pause. Then: "How is he? How is my Gregor?"

"Banged up, but he's been taken care of. We'll know more later."

Ozella wasn't satisfied. "Is he OK?"

Jessica clenched her jaw. "I don't know. I'm not a doctor."

A beat.

"Can I speak with him?"

"He's sleeping right now."

"I see." A longer pause. Then, relentless: "Can I speak with a doctor?"

"They're very busy, Ozella. I'll let Gregor know you called."

"And you'll get him to call back?"

"Sure."

Another pause. Then, clipped: "Fine. You will call if you hear anything more?"

"You bet."

And that was that. The phone went dead.

Gregor stirs awake again just after 8:30.

Jessica is by his side.

Her chair is pulled close, elbows resting on the bedside railings, head bowed in deep concentration. Dark purple bags hang beneath her beautifully intense, but exhausted, eyes.

Gregor follows her gaze.

The TV in the far corner is on. Volume low. Subtitles rolling.

She senses him watching. "Sorry," she murmurs. "I hope I didn't wake you."

"You didn't." His voice is hoarse. "What's this?"

"An update on the accident."

They fall silent, watching as the reporter stands on a verge overlooking the M25.

Traffic moves through the wreckage site now, but the road is still scarred. Deep, ugly tyre tracks slash across the tarmac, a permanent warning to anyone passing through. A reminder of how fast life can change.

The camera cuts to close-ups.

A smashed car mirror.

A burned alloy.

A scattering of glass, glinting in the weak morning light.

And then — a doll.

Abandoned in the lay-by.

Torn from the hands of the child who once held it.

Jessica exhales. "Would you believe there has been a Facebook page set up to try to reunite that doll with its owner?"

Gregor doesn't respond.

Can't respond.

He thinks how his future lies somewhere in that wreckage, buried among the debris.

As he does, he feels his chest tighten.

He's struggling to breathe.

The room begins to shrink.

His breaths grow shallow — sharp, rapid gulps of air that do nothing to fill his lungs.

Jessica is shouting.

The emergency button smacks against the wall.

Footsteps. Voices. A sudden rush of movement.

Doctors. Nurses. A flurry of hands and wires.

Gregor is surrounded.

Like a spectacle.

And moments later, Gregor's strapped up to a ventilator.

Apparently, it's not enough to be a quadriplegic.

Not enough that the basics of living — things he never even thought about — have become as impossible as solving a Rubik's cube blindfolded.

No.

Apparently, being this fucked also means his breathing is fucked too.

Gregor's losing control of his diaphragm.

The mask itches like hell, digging into the back of his head, catching in his thick hair. But he'll take that over the raw, suffocating panic of not being able to breathe. That had been something else.

Now, at least, he's stable.

He forces himself to take slow, deep breaths, following the lead of the older doctor standing over him. Inhale. Exhale. Deliberate. Measured.

Whenever Gregor has ever seen anyone doing this, he immediately thinks of Darth Vader.

I am your father.

Even now, he just can't help it. Gregor grew up on those films, watching Luke Skywalker start from nothing, a mere farm boy, to become the galaxy's only hope.

Those films made him feel like anything was possible.

Now, here he is.

Breathing like Vader, trapped in a body that no longer belongs to him.

Gregor keeps up the slow, rhythmic breathing as the doctor steps back.

To his left, Jessica speaks. "Any news on the scan results?"

"Not when I checked an hour ago," the doctor replies. "We're still expecting them today."

"An hour ago?" Jessica's voice sharpens. "Can you check again, please?"

"As soon as I've finished my rounds, it'll be the first thing I do. You have my word."

"Thanks."

Gregor knows that tone.

Jessica's got a bee in her bonnet.

Scratch that — she's got a whole fucking hive kicking off.

The doctor offers a polite, dismissive smile before disappearing out of Room 201.

Jessica scoffs. "What a twat. Seriously, all they've done is fob me off since we got here. How hard is it to get a few fucking results?"

Gregor tries to respond, but the mask is still clamped over his mouth. He makes a garbled attempt before Jessica clicks on and gently pulls it away.

He sucks in a breath, trying to form the words — trying to get something out to calm her down.

But before he can—

A shrill alarm blares from further down the corridor.

A few minutes later, the alarm stopped.

But the crying didn't.

A raw, piercing wail. Thick with grief. With loss. With the kind of despair that stripped a person bare.

Gregor had never heard anything like it.

And all he could do was lie there.

Listen.

Even after Jessica shut the door to Room 201, it didn't matter. The sound had already claimed every inch of the unit, soaking into the walls, seeping into the air like fresh paint.

She grabbed the remote, cranked the TV volume up, filling the room with meaningless chatter. Trying to drown the sound out.

But how do you drown something out that's now locked inside your brain?

Sometime after 3pm, Dr Oatney breezed into Room 201 and shut the door behind her, sealing them off from everything happening beyond the walls.

Just the three of them now.

And an excruciating ball of tension.

On the TV, a rerun of Flog It droned on. Gregor had never watched it before, but it was something — something to cut through the silence, to make the room feel a little less suffocating.

A flimsy attempt at normality.

He'd hoped it might help Jessica too. But as the hours dragged on, her frustration only deepened, simmering just beneath the surface. She wanted answers. She didn't understand the lack of urgency. Why wasn't anyone moving at *her* pace?

Dr Oatney's entrance came just in time to stop her from boiling over. Jessica grabbed the remote, killing the TV in anticipation.

They'd seen Dr Oatney before, rushing back and forth across the unit. But up close, she was strikingly tall — over six feet at least, Gregor thought. The next thing he noticed was how exhausted she looked. Eyes heavy. Shoulders tight with the weight of too many long shifts. Too many hard conversations.

Gregor wondered how many lives she'd had to dismantle since the accident.

"Sorry to keep you waiting," she says, a collection of multicoloured files clutched at her side.

Jessica didn't waste a second. "Do you have the test results?"

"I do."

Those two words.

Heavy. Measured. Carefully placed.

Gregor heard it instantly — the way her voice balanced on the thin edge of empathy.

He knew exactly how this was going to play out.

He'd braced himself for this, mentally preparing for the worst. But a small part of him — naïve, desperate — had still clung to hope.

Hope that while things were shit now, there was a way forward. Something that could be done to fix it.

Some treatment. Some surgery. Some *something*.

But with the passing of those two words, that hope shattered.

Jessica, either missing Dr Oatney's tone or refusing to accept it, leaned forward. "Well?"

But the doctor hesitated.

Gregor saw it in her face. The way she shifted slightly, as if reluctant to bring the hammer down on the flat head and knock it out of shape for extra measure. It didn't matter how long you did this job. Delivering news like this was never easy.

Gregor held his breath.

Dr Oatney exhaled.

"Gregor," she began carefully, "I'm really sorry to tell you that, based on the tests and examinations we've conducted, you've sustained a severe spinal cord injury as a result of the crash. It's an incomplete injury, but..." She hesitated, choosing her words. "It's complex. The CAT scan you had when you first arrived showed a significant fracture in your sixth cervical vertebra. The damage has compressed your spine."

The words hung in the air.

Heavy. Crushing.

Gregor felt like he was suffocating under them.

This wasn't new information, not really. But hearing it out loud? It sounded like a death sentence.

The invisible chains locking him in place weren't coming off.

Ever.

He turned to Jessica.

She wiped away a rogue tear, rolling her tongue over her top lip. Back and forth. Back and forth.

Then she spoke.

"I want a second opinion."

The words took Gregor aback.

"Jessica, what are you—"

She cut him off completely. All that bubbling away, Jessica had now reached boiling point.

"I want you to take your scans and get a fucking second opinion," she choked out, barely holding herself together. As if force — will — could change reality. As if being strong enough, angry enough, could somehow fix this.

But life didn't work that way.

Dr Oatney stepped back, hands up in quiet surrender. "Of course. I'm sorry."

"I don't want your sorry." Jessica's voice cracked, fists clenched. "I want you to make this fucking better."

5

Jessica's phone buzzes on the table.

She'd nipped to the loo and, for the first time in hours, left it behind.

The second she stepped away, Gregor exhaled.

Since the scan results, Jessica had thrown herself into research. Reading everything she could about spinal injuries. Searching for miracle stories — the one-in-a-million cases where someone defied the odds.

Refusing to accept that there was no solution.

He heard the tinny click of the bathroom bin before she emerged, scooping up her phone as she passed.

"I've had a text from Carl," she says. "He's asking if he can swing by around six."

Carl O'Rourke.

The guy Gregor wasn't sure about at first — loud, raucous, always on. The kind of person who never let a meeting finish without making sure his voice was the last one heard.

The kind of guy Gregor usually avoided.

Carl knew how to play the corporate game. He kissed the right arses, said the right things, and — annoyingly — got the best projects because of it. If there was an industry award bash, Carl's name was guaranteed to be on the guest list.

But Gregor had learned something important after a few sweaty, boozy after-work nights in London's underbelly.

Carl's bravado wasn't arrogance.

It was survival.

Architect firms were cutthroat. If work dried up, people got axed. And more often than not, it wasn't the best people who survived. It was the well-liked ones.

It wasn't what you knew. It was who.

And Carl?

Carl had been burned before.

So, he'd learned how to play the game. And to his credit, he wasn't just all talk — he was damn good at what he did. His ideas, his designs, could leave you feeling like there was no way in hell you'd ever come up with anything better.

And yet, beneath all the swagger, the charm, the cheeky grins, Carl was just a guy who wanted to be liked.

Now, he was like a brother to Gregor.

Jessica glanced at him. "You sure you're even up for visitors after today?"

"I think I could do with it, to be honest."

Her fingers tapped quickly across the screen, a quiet whoosh confirming the message had been sent.

"While he's here, you should get yourself home for a bit," Gregor says.

"Don't be daft. I've told you. I'm going—"

"Nowhere. I heard you." He sighs. "But... you've been here for days now. You haven't eaten properly, you haven't showered. And I'm sorry, but you're starting to smell a bit."

Jessica's eyes narrowed. "Fucker."

For the first time in hours, a flicker of something light passed between them. A rare, fleeting moment of ease.

Gregor smiled. “Go. Have a few hours to yourself. Freshen up. Clear your head. You’ll feel better for it.”

Out of the corner of his eye, Gregor saw the sun setting.

A sliver of dusky orange clung to the room, fighting against the inevitable pull of night.

Then came the knock.

Carl O’Rourke stood in the doorway.

Same thin brown hair, gelled into a point. Same chequered shirt over black jeans, cropped just above his bare ankles. Same smart loafers tying the look together.

The only difference was the look of sorrow etched into his features, replacing the usual happy façade.

But the usual cocky grin was missing.

Instead, his face was lined with something Gregor hated.

Pity.

“Fuck, man.”

A guy who was never lost for words... was struggling to find them.

Gregor wanted to skip this part. Fast-forward. Past the awkward glances, past the poor bastard expressions, straight to how things used to be. Joking. Laughing. Shooting the shit.

So, he forced a smirk. “Don’t just stand there. What you got for me?”

Carl hoisted up a bag — stuff Gregor knew would be from the Scale crew.

A card, signed by everyone.

Chocolates. Biscuits. Maybe a bottle of the good stuff.

They were a solid bunch at Scale. Always pitched in for birthdays, anniversaries, anything worth celebrating.

Carl set the bag down carefully, as if one wrong move might send it tumbling.

A beat of silence passed between them.

Carl hesitated.

Gregor sighed. *He needs help.*

"Well, come on then," he says, forcing a lightness into his voice. "Show me what's inside. Not sure you've noticed, but I'm a little incapacitated."

Carl snorted. "Duh. What a klutz."

Carl tears the tape apart and fumbles around the bag. He pulls out some of the usual stuff. A small box of Guylian, a bag of his favourite popcorn, a small teddy bear.

Then there's a lumberjack's cabin-scented candle... "to help get rid of that hospital smell. Not my idea for a gift."

"Claire?" Gregor guesses.

"Claire," Carl confirms with a grin.

And finally, a voucher for HelloFresh... "a little something for Jessica, too."

Carl pulled out the signed Get Well Soon card, flipping it over in his hands. And just like that, the easy rhythm between them stalled.

"Signed by everyone," he says, voice quieter now. "But yeah. You knew that."

He takes a seat, shifting it closer to the bedside. Lines up the card neatly against the vase of wilting chrysanthemums.

"Not the same in the office without you, dude."

Gregor smirked. "Better, is it?"

Carl laughs. Gregor laughed, too.

Then—

Gregor's chest tightened.

The laugh turned into a cough.

Then another.

Then — he couldn't catch his breath.

Carl shot to his feet, panic slamming into him like a freight train.

"HELP!" His voice thundered down the corridor.

Again. And again.

"I need HELP in here!"

The damn mask was back.

Strapped tight to his face.

His breathing had settled, but fuck, he hated this thing.

Alexandra Calloway had come to the rescue. She'd just clocked in for her night shift, looking fresh, ready to take on whatever the hospital threw at her.

She fiddled with the machine, tapping buttons, adjusting settings, her expression calm, practiced. The rhythmic hum and beep returned.

She turned to face him.

"And... rightyo. All set. New rule, Gregor. Blink once for yes and twice for no. Is there anything I can get you before I start my rounds."

He blinks twice.

"You want me to call your wife?"

Another two blinks.

"Grand. I'll leave you both to it then. Same goes for you...?"

She left the question hanging, turning to Carl.

"Carl."

"Carl. The less he talks, the better. Deal?"

Carl smirked. "Gotcha."

"That's what I like to hear." She winked. "Come find me if you need anything. I'll be around... somewhere."

And just like that, Alexandra was off.

Probably off to go and save more lives.

Carl watched her leave, eyes lingering a little too long as she wove down the corridor.

"She's nice," he mutters.

If Gregor could speak without choking, he'd rib him for it. Instead, he can only lie there and stare at his best friend.

"Want to hear about work?"

Yes. Yes. Yes.

Shame it's impossible to enthusiastically blink once.

But Carl didn't need much encouragement. Within minutes, he was back in his element — spinning long-winded, exaggerated stories, laughing at his own jokes, reminding Gregor for the hundredth time about how fit Claire was from HR.

Gregor needed this.

He was thankful for it.

Then—

"Oh, shit," Carl blurts. "I forgot to say, man. We won the Algorix contract."

Gregor's eyes widened.

The Algorix design.

His baby for the past month.

A plush office refurb on Old Street for a high-flying AI startup, fresh off a Series C funding round, convinced they were about to take over the world.

And they were going to do it from the space that *he* designed.

That was so fuckin' cool.

"Yeah, fuckin' great, isn't it? We sent the contract over earlier today. Knowing these guys, they'll have it signed and wrapped up by the end of this week."

A signed contract usually meant a bottle of something special for Gregor — a fresh bottle of Chateau La Tour-Haut-Brion's 1996.

Two large glasses.

Him and Jessica, toasting a big win.

The only way he'd be drinking it this time was through a straw.

If he could even manage that.

The thought cut him down instantly.

But Gregor kept his façade in place.

Didn't want Carl to see the anger bubbling under the surface. No point making him feel like shit.

But Carl had seen through it.

The room quieted.

Carl's grin faded.

He leaned forward, elbows resting on his knees, rubbing his palms together roughly. Head bowed. Back to how he was when he first walked in.

Then he spoke.

"Gregor... do you remember what happened, man?"

Gregor blinked twice.

6

Getting back to their flat in Lewisham was painful.

In more ways than one.

London traffic was *always* bad.

London traffic on a Friday night? *A fucking nightmare.*

The whole city was alive. Lights. Drinks. Food. Shows. Laughter.

People toasting another week survived.

Even in Jessica's little pocket of London, Deptford High Street was busy. A mixture of people dolled up, heading to the tube station to head over to Covent Garden, or Shoreditch, or Camden, or Soho — depending on what tickled their fancy.

Others didn't need to go far.

Some were content with a slow stroll down the street to the local — The Blue Moon.

Jessica's first job after moving to London.

The place where she'd met Gregor.

She pulled up outside their flat, locked her Micra.

Then just... stood there.

Staring at the door.

She couldn't go in. Not yet.

Her gaze drifted back to the small crowd heading for The Blue Moon.

Going about their lives.

Full of life.

Not a care in the world.

Unaware of how it can all be stripped away in the blink of an eye.

Jessica exhaled, her breath clouding in the cold night air.

She headed in the same direction.

"Well, look what the Lamb of God dragged in."

Rahul Varma. The rock-loving, shot-chasing MF who'd given Jessica a break when she first landed in Lewisham back in '08.

He rounds the bar and pulls her into a tight, one-armed hug, his forearm slick with faded tattoos. His chequered shirt stinks of stale ale and sweat. Some things never change.

"What the devil brings you here? No Gregor?"

She barely hears him over the juke kicking out an old Radiohead album.

"Not tonight and I just fancied going somewhere shit."

Rahul grins. "You'll be wanting the Wicked Boar down the road, then." She'd lost track of how many times he'd cracked that joke.

He leans against the bar, wiping his hands on a rag. "What can I get ya?"

"A small one?"

"Coming up. Take a seat. I'll join ya for five."

She takes a seat under a framed Van Halen vinyl – OU812.

Signed in white marker.

There were a few frames like this dotted around the place, but Jessica knew this one was Rahul's pride and joy. That and the old juke.

His love for rock went back to his teens. He'd told her about stumbling across his uncle's vinyl collection. How he'd pulled out Led Zeppelin IV one day and lost himself in the electrifying riffs and raw energy. He was never talented enough to make it himself — aside from the odd sloppy gig on a Friday night — but he'd always had another dream.

Owning a rock-themed pub.

And The Blue Moon had become his canvas, his very own vinyl sleeve he'd been able to dress to his taste. A space to turn into London's very own rock haven. A place to share his passion for heavy electric guitars and big beats.

It was also a shit hole.

But it was a well-loved shit hole.

Thursday to Saturday, it would be packed — locals squeezed in tight as some band with a corny name, bad clothes, and even worse moves took the floor. Jessica wouldn't be sticking around for that tonight, but for now, she was grateful for the company.

Rahul plants a small red in front of her before landing in the chair beside her with a heavy sigh. A Strongbow Dark Fruits within reach, the scent as rich and ripe as the colour. The table marked by the ghostly rings of pints that had come and gone.

Rahul takes a cloth from his shoulder and carelessly drops it between their drinks. Cleaning: it'll get done when it gets done... or when someone complains loud enough about it.

"It's been a while, girl. How have things been with the teaching?"

"Fine."

"Only fine. You left this place for only fine?"

"It's great."

"I hope you're more cheery in the classroom than you were here."

"Fuck you."

"You're a treat."

"And you're an ass."

They laugh, falling into reminiscing. Memories not as old as the vinyl on the walls, but still as vivid. Jessica hadn't sought this, but she realised she'd needed it.

She feels her phone buzz in her front pocket.

A text from Ozella. *Any news?*

"Anyone important?"

"Nah, just spam."

"Hate that shit."

"You're telling me."

Her eyes drift to the bar as a couple of punters move away. Behind them, a framed photo of a man with a collection bucket next to it.

"What's that over there?" she asks. "Someone looking for charity?"

"Not quite. You remember Notty?"

"As in Alex Nottson?"

Alex 'Notty' Nottson. A local carpenter. In every Friday or Saturday night with his wife, Trish. It had only just hit Jessica that she hadn't seen him tonight.

"That's the one. We're raising money for his family. Poor fucker died."

"Shit. What happened?"

"He was in that crash on the M25. Must've heard about it, right?"

"I did..." She left it there.

"Well, they got him outta his van and straight to the Spire East but he passed away yesterday from his injuries."

"That's..."

"Shit, ain't it?"

"Poor bastard."

And just like that, the illusion of normality shattered. The warmth of the bar, the scratchy thrum of Radiohead, the easy comfort of Rahul — it all faded. Her body was still here, but her mind was back in the hospital.

Back in Room 201.

"Rahul!" Some guy from behind the bar — someone Jessica didn't recognise. "Can you hold the fort while I change the Doom Bar keg?"

"Sure thing, Polly."

"Polly?" Jessica raised a brow.

"Ah, you never met Joel, did you? Good kid. Does a few shifts around his uni work. Surname's *Polgreen* — hence *Polly.* Hates it. We love it, though. Of course it stuck."

"Sounds about right."

"You sticking around?"

"Nah. Thinking I might go to The Wicked Boar for one."

Rahul fakes vomiting. "I'll bar you if you say shit like that again. I'll bring another over for you."

"Cheers, Rahul."

And back to business he went.

The Blue Moon had swelled and was gradually getting busier.

More bodies, more noise.

People kept filtering in, and barely anyone was leaving. A line snaked around the bar, another forming behind it — the kind that only ever appeared as the weekend crept closer.

Rahul held down one side. Polly the other.

Jessica had claimed a stool and high table as far from the crowd as possible.

She flicked through Facebook.

Scrolled through Instagram.

Checked old photos, old posts, old memories on her sisters' profiles, all while ignoring the calls and texts coming through from Ozella.

Another one came through. She clicked the phone shut and shoved it into her handbag. Rubbed at the corners of her tired, itchy eyes.

She felt gross.

Made the decision that she was going to head back to the flat soon and grab a shower.

Another thought crisscrossed her mind.

She stuck her hand back into her bag.

Ferreted around for the phone.

Not her phone. Gregor's.

The Galaxy screen was cracked, the case scuffed and peeling. A little worse for wear, but a survivor from the M25 crash.

She turned it on.

Tapped in the password. Her birthday.

A series of messages and notifications came flooding through.

Ping, ping, ping.

She ignored them.

Scrolled straight to the messages.

Under her own name — an unfinished text.

She taps through.

The cursor blinked, waiting.

What bout that French plac

Jessica had seen it before.

She knew what Gregor was like behind the wheel.

But seeing the unfinished message now — again — sent a deep shiver through her skin, sharp enough to make her arms prickle.

And the thought — no, the fear — that had been gnawing at her all night?

It wasn't going anywhere.

7

That night, Gregor dreamt of home again.

Except this time, it was as though his unconscious had hit the play button and picked back up where it had left off the night before.

He was back in the car with Arek.

Out on the country roads, taking the short drive out to Lake Łagowskie for a camping trip.

Dusk settling in, the sky a deep purple wash.

They were on the DK92 motorway, slipping between slower drivers, cutting through a collage of red taillights. Each time Arek overtook, he threw up a middle finger and marked the moment with a swig from his beer.

Republika's blaring out the system. Gregor's bobbing his head along, guzzling his second can, psyched for a night under the stars with the boys.

Arek turns off to 1236F.

Takes another swig. A big one that takes his eyes off the road momentarily.

Not concentrating.

Gregor has to pull the wheel as he nearly crosses over onto a slim grass verge, just past a sign for the village of Gronów.

"Cholernie blisko," Arek says, laughing. Unfazed.

Damn close.

They drive a little further.

The cassette clicked to a stop. Gregor reached for the eject button, but Arek slapped his hand away.

"I've got it."

His beer can sits between his legs as he fiddles with a box packed full of cassettes.

Not concentrating on the road ahead again.

This time, they weren't speeding down the motorway.

This time, they were on the main artery of a village. Slower streets. Fewer lights.

They're in Gronów, just a few kilometres from Łagów and the turnoff for the lake.

They pass a bus stop on Gregor's right, a small fenced-in well a few metres further down the road.

Neither of them sees the bike coming out of the side street.

Not until it's too late.

Gregor sees it first. "Gówno!"

Shit.

Arek yanks hard on the wheel, veering off to the left.

The car smashes through chicken wire fencing.

Hits a mound of dirt.

Launches into the air.

A sickening crash.

The windshield explodes into a million jagged shards as the car flips onto its side — then rolls, hard, back onto its wheels.

When Gregor wakes, the first thing he saw was Arek's eyes.

Looking deep into his.

Empty.

Dead.

The room was semi-dark when Gregor's eyes fluttered opened.

Moonlight sliced through the blinds, a dim torch casting pale streaks across the walls. From the corridor, the hazy glow of LEDs near the reception desk offered the only other source of light.

Somewhere down the unit, a low hum of conversation drifted through the air. The quiet rattle of medicine bottles on a trolley followed.

Gregor craned his neck, just enough to glimpse the clock.

Just past three in the morning.

Where's Jessica?

The chair she'd occupied for the past few days sat pulled up against his bedframe — empty.

Her phone lay face down on the bedside table, next to a half-filled jug of water.

Then something catches his eye.

Back out in the corridor.

The lights flickered.

Once.

Twice.

The chatter he'd heard ceases.

The voices he'd heard stopped mid-sentence.

Silence.

And yet — he could still hear it.

A sound.

A shuffle.

A figure, moving unsteadily toward the entrance of Room 201.

Gregor's breath stalled in his throat.

His chest tightened.

Into the sliver of moonlight, the figure wandered.

A face emerged.

A face Gregor knew.

A face he had only seen in nightmares for the past sixteen years.

Arek.

But not exactly Arek.

His eyes — glossy, glazed, the colour of onyx.

The cheeky smile Gregor had grown up with was gone.

Replaced by straight-cut, emotionless lips.

Gregor's lungs burned. His body refused to move.

Arek stopped at the foot of the bed.

Stared down at him.

Then spoke.

One word.

"Remember."

The sound fizzled, like a dying ember in the air —

— and Gregor's world turned as black as his dead friend's eyes.

It comes in flashes.

Like a fractured movie, cutting out all the fillers and keeping all the important parts.

But the picture's blurry still.

The laughs.

The music.

The close shave after turning onto Gronów.

Swerving to avoid the bike that shot out from the side street.

Colliding with the man-made mud mountain.

The car flipping.

The crunch of metal devouring metal.

A cloud of charred smoke blooming from beneath the crumpled hood.

His best friend beside him.

Neck broken.

Eyes open.

Gazing into his soul,

Not from the driver's seat.

From the passenger's.

"Greg, wake up," says the woman's voice. "Come on. You're not fucking doing this. Not now."

He's flat on his back.

The damn oxygen mask is wrapped around the bottom of his face again.

On one side, Alexandra. On the other, Jessica.

"Oh, thank fuck. Thank fuck." Jessica says in between sobs.

But Gregor's not looking at her as she kisses his forehead and brushes a smooth thumb over his cheek.

No.

He's looking at Arek, who's standing at the end of his bed.

Those dead, onyx eyes locked onto him like a brand searing into his mind.

"Remember," he says again.

DAY 4

8

His eyes were closed.

Not asleep, just resting.

Gregor felt wrecked from the night — a night of disturbing dreams that left him fighting for every breath.

A fight he would have lost but for the ventilator that had needed to be strapped back on for a few hours again.

But it was just a dream.

Wasn't it?

He was mulling that question over when he latched on to a conversation sweeping into Room 201 from the corridor, like a tide flowing in and then back out before returning with more force. Usually, Gregor didn't pay hospital conversations much attention, but when he heard Jessica's voice getting increasingly animated, he couldn't help but eavesdrop.

The chatter had started at a low volume.

"Please, he's sleeping and had a rough night. Can't this wait until the afternoon at the least?"

That was Jessica. No doubt about it.

"I'm sorry about that, Ms Johnson. I am. But we really can't hold this off any longer," a male voice protested.

On it had gone a little while. Back and forth. Jessica was unrelenting. Whoever was out there with his wife was equally stubborn.

And then Jessica's voice began to raise, carrying that stinging frustration that Gregor had seen erupt occasionally over the last few days with the doctors and nurses.

Jessica. Impulsive, sure. But very rarely lost her shit around other people. He hated seeing how much this was messing her up. How much she was struggling under the weight of pressure.

"I've told you already... he doesn't remember anything about what happened."

"And while we appreciate that, we really need to ask him some other questions."

"What are you possibly hoping to learn? It was a fuckin' accident."

"Ms Johnson, please."

"Come back later!"

Another voice joins the fray — a woman's.

There is a little more back and forth, the argument returning to hushed tones.

And then a brisk knock on the door.

Two uniforms flank past Jessica.

Police officers: one man, one woman.

"Mr Johnson," the man starts. "How are you feeling?"

"I've been better," Gregor says. The response is coming out like it's part of a script. The standard pithy response to a redundant question. A question that those asking know the answer to.

"We're sorry to have to do this now."

"Come in. It's fine."

"I'm Detective Winslow. This is my partner, Detective Kestrel."

On first inspection, Winslow certainly was the older of the two. Late 40s, Gregor thought. A guy with a hard face under thin salt and pepper hair. A moustache the same colour that scratched the top of his lip. Cobalt-blue eyes sat beneath the first signs of wrinkles.

To his left, Kestrel was a looker — understated. Coal-black hair was pinned into a bun that, once released, he imagined would flow past her shoulders. Held up, though, it gave her a harsh edge. Beneath it, big hazel eyes studied him, unwavering. She was short and trim, no more than 5'5". A clean, well-maintained face, but not one you'd want to get on the wrong side of. The kind of face that told you, if a good cop/bad cop routine played out, she'd play the latter.

Jessica peeled off around to the unfamiliar left side, chewing at the cuticles on her thumb. That left the two uniforms to occupy the seats to Gregor's right.

"We were hoping to ask you some questions about the accident four days ago," Winslow says. "See what you remember about the event?"

"It's hazy, but let's give it a shot," Gregor says.

"Let's start with before. What had your day looked like? Where were you coming back from on that day?"

Jessica snaps, anger sharp in her voice.

"We know," Winslow says, curtly. "We're just dotting our I's and crossing the T's."

"It's fine, Jess," Gregor adds.

Jessica shakes her head and continues to gnaw at her thumb.

Gregor turned back to Winslow and Kestrel and walked them

through his day. A predictable, normal day in the office. A completely ordinary, bog-standard Tuesday. He told them about the project he was working on, where he got lunch, leaving the office at 4:30 on the dot. He told them about the thick fog that had set in. The spit of rain. How he crept onto the M25 off Bignell's Corner.

How the last sign he remembers seeing was for the upcoming turnoff for Lee Valley Park.

"And then nothing?" Winslow asks.

"Bits have come back from immediately after," Gregor says.

Jessica shoots him a look. The *well, this is news to me* kind.

Gregor turned back to Winslow. "I remember waking up. It had to be a little later because the first thing I saw was flashing sirens. There was smoke, so thick you saw it through the fog."

The smell and taste of it hit him again, sharp and bitter.

"There was a lot of shouting, too. Lotta bodies on the floor. Blood over by one of the cars that had been flipped up."

Winslow just looked at him through a lens of sympathy. Kestrel remained the same as when she walked through the door. Totally unreadable.

"And that was it. I was gone again."

"Anything a little while after."

"Nothing. Next time I woke up was here and two days had passed."

Winslow nodded, then leaned forward. "Let's go back a little — to when you were driving. Even before you saw the sign for Lee Valley Park. Do you recall seeing anyone driving erratically?"

"How so?"

"Maybe someone going too fast for the conditions. Maybe someone you thought was all over the place."

"Not that I can think of, no."

"That's fine," Winslow looks visibly disappointed with the response. Like he was expecting more. "K," he turns to his partner — bad cop. "Anything to add?"

Before she can answer, Gregor can't help himself. "Why'd you ask that? It was just an accident, wasn't it?"

"We're just trying to get a clear picture of what led to what happened," Winslow says.

Kestrel took over now. "I do have one question. Do you have your phone with you by any chance?"

"My phone?"

"Yeah."

Gregor hadn't seen it. Hadn't even thought about it, with everything else that had happened.

He turned to Jessica. "Was anything passed to you when I came in?"

She shook her head. "Only the clothes you were cut from, your wedding ring, and your wallet. Perhaps it's still at the crash site?"

"We'll be sure to check that, Ms Johnson."

"How would that help?" Gregor asks.

Detective Kestrel snapped her notebook shut. Leaned forward, her expression focused and determined.

"The reason we asked about your phone is that it might provide some insight into what happened. Often, mobile phone records can help us reconstruct events leading up to an accident. It's a standard part of our investigation."

Silence thickened the room.

Until Jessica cut through it. "So, is that everything?"

"For now," Winslow says, rising to his feet. "Thank you for your time."

He places a card on the desk. "If anything comes back to you — even the smallest detail — you can call me."

"Thank you. I'm sorry I couldn't be more help."

Winslow nods with a small smile. Kestrel doesn't even give him that.

And as Gregor watches them leave Room 201 behind, a motionless shadow caught his attention in the corridor.

As the detectives stepped beyond the frame, it replaced them — flickering into the room in a blurred motion.

Arek.

And he had the same message for Gregor from the night just gone.

Remember.

9

Winslow took a long sip of his coffee, wincing slightly as the heat burned the roof of his mouth. Worth it. His brain needed the caffeine. He could feel the morning already running away from him, slipping through his fingers like sand.

Kestrel leaned against the vending machine, arms crossed, eyes fixed on some distant thought. She had that look — the one she got when something didn't sit right.

"You think Johnson's holding back?" Winslow asks, setting his cup down and rubbing a hand over his stubbled jaw.

"Not sure," Kestrel admits. "But I do think there's more to dig into."

Winslow huffed a short laugh. "There always is." He swirled what was left of his coffee, watching the liquid spin like a whirlpool.

"You not having one?"

"Past time for me."

"Suit yourself. So, you're even more sure your hunch is right, yeah?"

"Think so. You think the wife knows more?"

"Yeah," Winslow agrees, rubbing the back of his neck. "She was wound up tight."

He thought she certainly seemed nervous, like she wanted to get them out of the room as soon as possible.

Maybe it was nothing.

But, perhaps, there was a reason.

Winslow and Kestrel had been immediately appointed on the M25 accident case. While everyone around them — victims, family, media, even other officers back at HQ — had labelled what had happened as a tragic accident, Winslow had been careful not to use that word.

To use the word accident implies that no one was at fault.

And throughout Winslow's career, the term accident fell into the same category that everyone used for innocent until proven otherwise.

Winslow only deemed something an accident once every other alternative was ruled out.

It was easy to see why everyone would think that was the case this time.

It is true, the fog that had descended that late Tuesday afternoon had been as thick as cotton candy. Winslow was a big Stephen King nut — he'd read 62 of his books to date and counting — but driving through it himself, it had reminded him of The Mist, a novella where a heavy mist smothered a small town in Maine and disguised the monsters that picked off the inhabitants one by one.

The novella was good. The film, not so.

Sure, no monsters had been involved in what happened on the M25, but the scene when he and Kestrel had arrived was certainly otherworldly.

He'd seen accidents and pile-ups and plenty of them.

But nothing like this.

Winslow let out a slow breath. He'd learned a long time ago that gut instinct was just as valuable as forensic evidence, and right now, his gut was telling him something wasn't adding up.

The M25 pile-up had looked chaotic, but if you peeled back the layers, if you examined the fractures and breaks in the sequence of events, there was something unnatural about it.

Someone, somewhere, had fucked up and fucked up badly.

It might have even only been something small, but someone had taken liberties in dangerous weather and pulled everyone around them into the shit pit.

Within that shit pit, there had been people that weren't getting out alive.

Over the last four days, Winslow and Kestrel had devoted themselves to solving the M25 mystery, all while everyone else around them just wanted this thing wrapped up with a neat bow and get it consigned to history.

No need to dig deep, it's *just* an accident.

No sirree.

Amongst the carnage of a traffic collision, especially no ordinary traffic collision, where the fuck do you start? Simple — you tick off the most obvious causes.

Fell asleep at the wheel? Maybe.

Drink driving? Another possibility.

Speeding? Unlikely in that fog, you'd be playing roulette with your life.

"Maybe they were distracted," Kestrel had suggested.

That was all Winslow had needed. He got her straight onto the cell tower records while he dealt with the unfurling chaos at East Spire Hospital.

By the time he arrived, a few hours after arranging for the crash site to be cleared and the roads shut, six were dead.

Over the last few days, that number had grown to 10.

Plenty of tears. Plenty of broken families.

Not a whole lot of answers.

Until yesterday.

Winslow had just wrapped up a morning of interviews when Kestrel wheeled over to his desk, wafting a thin folder in his face.

"What's this?"

"Take a look."

He had.

Kestrel had pulled the phone data for everyone involved in the crash. And there, circled in bright yellow, was a single text sent to a number belonging to Jessica Johnson.

Sent just before the accident.

"You think he was lying in there?" Kestrel asks, as she settles into her chair across from Winslow. The waiting room was quieter this morning. Quieter than it had been over the last few days.

"Not sure about that one. The chats I've had with the doctors looking after him suggest he really doesn't remember much."

"Convenient."

"Ever the cynic."

"We going to question Jessica?"

"I think we'd better."

And just at that moment, an alarm begins blaring from one of the rooms on the ward.

A stampede of feet, a fleet of doctors in blue overalls, head in the direction.

Right towards the siren.

A siren that would later lead to the death toll ticking to 11.

10

"Jess, wait — where are you —"

"I've got to take care of something. I'll be back soon."

She was gone before Gregor could muster another word.

Something was off.

She'd looked nervous the moment the detectives sat down by his bed. After they left, she'd barely spoken. Distracted. He could practically hear the cogs turning as she gnawed at the top of her right thumbnail.

The way she always did when something was eating away at her.

Gregor had shouted after her, but once Jessica was out the door and out of sight, there was nothing more he could do.

He was immediately left with something else to think about.

That being his dead best friend.

Arek was still here, lurking in the corner of his hospital room, an unwelcome presence occupying space that wasn't his to take.

Gregor squeezed his eyes shut. *Not real. Not real. Not real.*

But Arek was still there, a grotesque echo of the past — motionless, mouth bloodied, black eyes piercing through him.

"Remember."

Gregor clenched his jaw. The memories he'd locked away, buried deep for decades, pushed their way to the surface.

That late afternoon in Gronów.

Him and Arek laughing, sipping warm, bitter lager.

Cruising along the road, carefree.

Then—

A wreck.

Arek's dead eyes staring.

Blood dripping from his head, pooling on the dashboard, soaking into tiny shards of shattered windscreen.

"Remember."

The memories change. Alter. History comes together in a head-on collision with the very recent past.

Gregor remembers leaving the office. He sees it vividly. He and Claire crossing the car park, hugging, going their separate ways.

"Have a good evening."

"You, too."

Key turns. The Polo coughs to life. His Spotify playlist blares out the speakers and he turns the nozzles down.

Then, the fog. It's there. Not as thick or menacing as he remembers at first.

But present nevertheless.

He was singing along to T.Love, tapping the wheel, drumming his fingers.

Merging onto the M25.

The fog thickened, swallowing the road, smothering everything in an eerie cloak.

"Remember."

Traffic moving at a steady pace.

He's hugging the left lane behind a Fiesta, boredom beginning to creep in.

He thought of Jessica. Of popping open a bottle, clinking to what he feels has been a successful pitch for the Algorix contract. Of using the moment to talk, to fix whatever had been fraying between them.

"Remember."

First, he called.

Voicemail.

A sharp exhale.

Then he texted.

On my way back. I was thinking we could go out tonight x

Send.

"Remember."

A quick glance up at the road.

Then back down.

His wrist pressed into the steering wheel, keeping it steady.

The quicker he typed, the quicker he could be done. The quicker he could focus. Jessica would be excited — a date night, a reset.

His thumbs pounded across the screen.

He never noticed the car drifting.

Never noticed the tanker.

What about that French plac—

Then — chaos.

"Remember."

11

It was grim, really.

That someone else's death had given Jessica the window she needed to slip out of the hospital.

Out of sight while those two cops were distracted.

She had to move. Fast.

The sour-faced female detective's final question — about Gregor's phone — had left Jessica feeling sick.

Like a thief caught red-handed, her greedy hands buried in the till.

They know. Of course they fuckin' know.

The only reason they would ask about Gregor's phone is because they knew he'd sent a text from it while he'd been driving. If they know that's the case, they know he could have had something to do with what happened out on the M25.

Jessica wasn't sure herself if that's what had happened. Not exactly.

But she couldn't take the risk.

She needed to get rid of it.

Before they got their hands on it.

Before they used it to pin this all on Gregor.

She power-walked out of the unit, her heart hammering.

Then she ran.

Flats slapping against the resin floor, echoing down the corridor.

Labouring eyes flicked toward her.

She ignored them.

By the time she reached the car, her breath was short, her pulse a snare drum.

She climbed in, slammed the door, and tore off back to Lewisham.

The moment she hit the open road, Jessica smacked the steering wheel.

Once.

A few seconds passed.

Then again.

And again.

She sucked in a breath, biting her bottom lip until it stung — tasting the faint sweetness of the balm she'd smoothed on that morning.

This feeling. She knew it too well.

It took her straight back to the 24 hours after she'd fled Aston Orphanage at sixteen — running from her past and a dead body of a man who had it coming. She'd escaped under the disguise of the night and followed her plan right to the letter.

She'd spent every second looking over her shoulder.

Waiting to be caught.

Right up until she'd stepped onto the ferry, crossed the channel, and found the safety of Ireland's open arms.

Only now, instead of glancing behind her, she was glued to the rearview mirror.

Waiting.

For the sirens.

For the flashing lights.

For the moment they'd pull her over to the side of the road and wave a warrant in her face.

Come on, Jessica. We know you've got it. Now, hand it over.

She forced herself to breathe. To focus.

To do what she'd always had to.

What needed to be done.

Her phone starts vibrating just as she pulls up outside the flat.

Jessica's first thought is that it's the hospital.

When she sees the name, she'd wished it had been.

Ozella.

Shit.

One problem at a time. She can't afford any distractions.

She hits the lock button and stuffs it back in her coat pocket, letting it ring out as she scampers up the stairs towards the flat door.

Inside, she drops her bag by the rack of coats and heads through the second door on the left and straight to the bedroom.

She crouches down beside the bedside table. Beneath it, rolled up in an orange plastic Co-op bag, is Gregor's phone.

Jessica moves fast. Memory card out. SIM out. Both disappear into her coat pocket, joining her own phone. Then she grabs

Gregor's Samsung and heads for the lounge.

She drops it onto the slate carpeted floor with a dull thud.

Looks around.

She needs something heavy. Something final.

Her eyes land on the white stone-carved Relax sign she'd bought from Camden market for the coffee table.

That'll do it.

Jessica grips it tight and brings it down. Hard.

Crack.

She swings again.

Again.

Again.

Shards of glass scatter like tiny ice slivers, vanishing into the carpet's dense curls. The front casing splits wide open, exposing delicate circuitry beneath.

She takes a step back, breathes.

Gone.

Now she just has to get rid of the rest.

It takes Jessica 11 minutes to drive over Deptford Creek.

Midweek means no trouble finding a parking spot outside the Creekside Discovery Centre. She steps out into the cool autumn air, the breeze picking up, clouds darkening by the second.

Fitting, for this part of town.

Graffiti-stained walls — most of it old and faded. Pavements lined with waste. The distinct, pungent whiff of weed drifting from the rundown block of flats across the road.

Jessica turns back toward the viaduct that looms over Creekside, slipping into an alley beside it. Follow the road through, and it'll spit you out at the A200. She'll be heading that way soon — back to the hospital — once she's taken care of business here.

The alley is a riot of colour, a world apart from the scribbled tags and crude murals she passed moments ago. Bright, chaotic, surreal. Big words, big creatures, bold strokes of paint tangled together in a fever dream that stretches the length of the walkway, weeds and rubbish trailing underneath.

A train thunders overhead. A sharp blast of its horn makes her jump.

She exhales, slow and measured. Still on edge. Still tracking every movement around her.

No one's following.

But paranoia won't loosen its grip.

She pushes on. A few minutes later, she reaches the small bridge that spans the creek. The royal blue paint is splintered, rust bleeding through.

Jessica steps to the edge. Wind tugs at her hair as she looks down.

Brown, murky water. The kind you find anywhere in the UK. But here, in this forgotten corner of the city, it just makes sense.

She scans her surroundings again. Not just left and right — the way she came — but everywhere. Checking for prying eyes. For anyone who might talk to the wrong people about what they're about to see.

Satisfied, she reaches into her coat pocket and pulls out the Co-op bag. Inside, Gregor's phone lies in unrecognisable pieces.

Jessica turns back to the creek and shakes the bag out over the water, flicking it up and down to make sure every shard falls.

Gone.

She watches for a second. Then chucks in one-half of Gregor's memory card. The rest — excessively cut-up — gets scattered into separate bins on the way back to the car.

The Co-op bag, too.

Then, it's back to the hospital.

The problems just kept on coming.

A crash outside Deptford grinds traffic to a halt, making the drive back to Spire East London Hospital a painful crawl.

Jessica drums her fingers against the wheel, jaw tight. The line of cars ahead isn't moving when she feels the buzz of her phone against her hip.

She fishes it out.

More missed calls from Ozella.

And now a text.

A hornet's nest of anxiety stirs in her stomach as she swipes to open it.

How could you lie to me? I have spoken to the hospital and they've told me EVERYTHING that has happened. I've always known you're a piece of work, a piece of shit. Bad for my son. I am catching a flight to England right now. You will not keep me away any longer.

Jessica's teeth grind. Heat rises up her throat.

But it's not enough to stop her from stinging her palm against the steering wheel again and screaming into the void.

12

It happened again.

Gregor had shit himself. And he hadn't even known.

A couple of days ago, back when he'd believed a random, cruel twist of fate had robbed him of feeling from the neck down, he'd fixated on the small details — like how the hell he'd manage something as simple as going to the toilet.

Now he knew.

It wasn't a cruel twist of fate. It wasn't random.

It was his own goddamn fault.

And now, this. The simplest act — taking a dump in peace, doom-scrolling on his phone, wiping his own ass — gone. Taken for granted his whole life, now forever out of reach.

Never mind doom-scrolling. Never again would he be able to take a shit without someone else cleaning him up afterward.

Like a fucking baby that didn't know any better.

Gregor stared at the sterile wall, a silent witness to his unravelling pride. His jaw tight while Alexandra and another nurse — his ego was too battered to even catch her name — set about restoring whatever dignity they could. On the table, more petals had fallen from the vase of chrysanthemums he'd woken up to two days ago.

Even through his humiliation, one thought pressed its way to the front of his mind.

Arek.

Remember.

What really happened out on the M25?

Gregor needed to talk to Jessica.

When the nurses finished, he asked whether either of them had seen his wife. It had been a couple of hours since Jessica had disappeared flustered and in a hurry after the police had spoken with them that morning, but Alexandra said she hadn't.

When Gregor was finally changed and settled back into the bed, the nurse with Alexandra took herself off with the cleaning apparatus without saying a word. Probably sensed there was nothing she could say that would make a 36-year-old quadriplegic feel any less like shit about shitting himself.

Alexandra lingered, tidying up, uncharacteristically quiet.

She looked... weighed down.

Like someone with the whole world pressing against her back.

Like how Gregor felt.

"Everything ok?" He asks.

"Not really," Alexandra says, her voice heavy with something deeper than exhaustion.

"Wanna talk?"

Her eyes welled instantly. She blinked hard, fighting it, but Gregor could see the cracks forming.

"I lost someone today," she says, not pausing her work. Even now, duty came first.

"I'm sorry." A tired old cliché. Useless, but all he had.

Alexandra exhaled. "Remember that trip around Poland I told you about?"

Gregor nodded.

"He — Jamie, his name was Jamie — was part of that."

"What happened?"

"The same as you."

Gregor felt it immediately. A crushing weight in his gut, like a shot of sambuca going down wrong.

The heavy realisation setting in that his mistake impacted more than just him.

"He was driving back from a meeting with his publisher. He'd written a children's book. Had been working on it for a couple of years on and off. He had his idea for it while we were travelling. We're all in this WhatsApp chat and I still remember the day he told us it was being published by Puffin."

Gregor swallowed. "What was it about?"

Alexandra wiped at her cheek, smudging mascara. "It's called *The Dreamer*. I only got to see a page or two, but it's about a boy who can live in the worlds he dreams up. Then he finds himself trapped in a nightmare. He meets a monster — big, scary-looking thing — but it turns out it's all in the boy's head. Together, they go on an adventure to escape the nightmare and return to the boy's dreams."

Words dessert Gregor. What the hell was there he could say?

She hesitated, voice growing thick. "Publishing that book, seeing it on the shelves at Waterstones or The Works, in people's hands... that was his dream. He'll never get to see it."

Alexandra lingered by the bedside.

"But you know what Jamie dreamed of more?" she said finally. "Reading that book to his son."

Gregor felt his stomach twist.

Alexandra pauses by his bedside before continuing.

"Turned 3 last month, he did. He's a cheeky little so-and-so. Full of personality and energy. Can't take your eyes off him for a second. He, Lucas, was born here. I was on shift when his girlfriend gave birth."

A fleeting smile crossed her face. Then it was gone, like she was reminding herself she wasn't allowed to feel happy right now.

"He's just getting to the age where he actually engages with books," she continued. "Not just flicking through the pages or throwing them across the room."

A single tear slipped down her cheek. Then another.

Gregor had never wanted kids. Never felt that pull.

But now, he thought about Lucas. A boy growing up without his dad.

A boy waiting on his bed, book in hand, looking at the door.

Waiting for his father to come in, tuck him in, read to him.

The way Gregor's dad used to.

Gregor feels a warm tear of his own tickle the side of his nose.

"I'm sorry," Gregor says again. But it felt smaller now. More hollow.

Alexandra wiped at her cheek, eyes red-rimmed but dry. "Life," she murmured. "It can be so damn cruel sometimes."

13

It's just gone 12 when Jessica steps through the automatic doors of Spire East London Hospital, leaving the brewing weather behind her.

She's entered from the main entrance this time — right at the opposite end to where the Intensive Care Unit is. Not her usual route, but she needs coffee and food, and with Costa and M&S side by side, this is as good as it gets once you're inside these walls. There's nothing else within walking distance.

She grabs a couple of meal deals, taps through the self-checkout, and then joins the sluggish queue at Costa. It's moving at a snail's pace — understaffed as usual — but she's committed now.

The wait starts her off, thinking of Ozella again, trying to weigh up when Gregor's dragon of a mother is going to be landing at Gatwick.

How long had she got before she was going to have to deal with the bitch in person?

Jessica pulls out her phone and turns to the old reliable — Google.

Time's on her side. Ozella's text had come in about an hour ago, around 11, saying she was catching a flight "*right now.*" If that was true, she wouldn't be landing at Gatwick until at least 5. And that was if there were no delays.

Then there was security. Baggage claim — assuming she'd even packed a suitcase. A taxi. Wading through rush-hour traffic. Then figuring out where Gregor was inside one of London's biggest hospitals.

She might not actually be at the hospital until after 7.

Well, at least that's something.

"Where've you been?"

Gregor spits the words out the second Jessica pushes through the door, closing it behind her. A large coffee is clutched in one hand.

If he could, he'd be on his feet, pacing, gesturing — Gregor was that kind of guy. Someone who stood when his back was up, who couldn't just sit when things turned rough. He was all about active engagement, not passive submission.

But this was a new reality.

"I told you, there was something I needed to deal with," she says. A hint of defensiveness leaks through her tone.

"Something that took you more than a couple of hours?"

"It was important, ok. What am I getting the third degree for?"

Jessica's words land with a mix of exasperation and something else — guardedness.

Gregor exhales sharply, frustration tightening his chest. "I—ahhh."

A thick tension settles between them. Heavy. Unspoken. It fills the room like a storm cloud too heavy to break.

Gregor watches her, searching. And somewhere in the silence, a terrifying thought creeps in.

Does she already know? Did she suspect this all along?

His heart races, hammering against his ribs. His ears ring with it, a deep, resounding drumbeat of anxiety and anticipation.

In the corner of the room, *he* is there.

Arek. Watching. Coal-black eyes fixed on him, unreadable. Urging him on.

Gregor swallows hard.

"I remember everything," he says, voice hushed, trembling.

Gregor unravels it all in a desperate whisper.

Jessica sits in her usual chair by the bed, hunched over, elbows pressing into her knees, hands clasped tight on the edge of his mattress. Taking it all in. Her face stays locked in concentration, revealing nothing. Not a flicker of emotion. Not a hint of what she's thinking.

He finishes with the weight that has been crushing him — something even heavier than the accident itself.

"Eleven people, Jess. Eleven people."

He repeats it. Again. And again. As though saying it once isn't enough to make it real. "They're dead because of something I did."

She grinds her teeth, digesting the magnitude of it. Her eyes trail off, as though the answer she is seeking is somewhere out the window. But no words pass her slightly parted lips.

"Please. Say something. What are we going to do?"

"I'm thinking."

"Thinking? What's there to think about? We... we have to tell the police."

She shakes her head.

Gregor's pulse kicks up. *"Jess, come on."* He urges her, desperate for an answer, an alternative, a way out of the mess he can't see past.

"We're not telling the police."

Still, she won't look at him. Or rather, she can't. Not directly, anyway. Just a glance into his eyes before diverting her gaze back towards the window. Whatever's turning over in her mind, she's not letting him in.

This morning, when the police were in Room 201, she had been flustered, struggling to keep her emotions in check. But now? Now, she's still. A quiet storm.

Gregor wants to reach out, to touch her arm, to pull her attention back to him.

But he can't.

Jessica pushes herself up from the chair, its plastic legs scraping against the resin floor. She moves around to the other side of the bed, arms crossed, one hand drifting to her mouth as she chews the edge of her thumb. Again.

"We have to."

Softly spoken. But firm.

Now, she finally turns to face him.

"I'm part of this now, too."

Jessica tells him about his phone.

How she'd found it waiting for her at the hospital, sealed inside one of those sterile, clear plastic bags. Still intact. Still alive and kicking. Not a single scratch to show it had been in the crash.

But the problem with phones isn't what's on the outside.

She had unlocked it easily — Gregor's PIN code was second nature to her. And the phone had picked up right where it left off.

The first thing she'd seen was the text.

And the unfinished one beneath it.

It hadn't taken a genius to work it out. The TV reporters were saying the fatal M25 crash had happened just after 5:30.

Gregor's phone showed he'd sent a text just after 5:31.

Jessica had thought about all the times they'd been in the car together. Short trips. Long trips. Date nights. Drives to the beach. To the hills. All those times he'd texted family, friends, colleagues — one hand on the wheel, the other glued to his phone.

Country roads. City streets. Motorways. It didn't matter. If Gregor's phone buzzed, he *wouldn't* — *couldn't* — just wait.

She thought about the near misses. The times he'd lingered on a message too long and nearly clipped a curb. Drifted too close to the central reservation.

So many times he'd got away with it.

So many times it could have happened sooner.

But it happened now.

And it had cost *many, many* others their lives.

"Where are you going?"

Gregor's voice is strained, desperate, as Jessica snatches up her coat and heads for the door. He wishes she'd stop leaving without saying anything.

"I need to think."

"Jess!" he calls after her again, but the coughing fit that follows swallows the rest of his words. The door clicks shut behind her, and that's the end of it.

Jessica doesn't stop. Doesn't turn back. The last thing she needs is more attention on Gregor when he's being so irrational.

As she strides down the corridor towards the waiting area, she spots the two police officers who had spoken to them earlier that morning. They're talking to a nurse — Gregor's regular one, she thinks. Alice? Alex? Something like that. The name evades her.

She's not as chirpy now. Arms folded. Head tipped back against the wall. The officers take notes as she speaks.

Jessica's stomach knots.

The only thing she tells herself is that they're talking about her and Gregor.

Without missing a beat, she pivots, turning in the opposite direction. There's a smaller waiting area ahead, a carved-out box space, barely big enough for a family. Opposite that, the disabled toilet.

Vacant.

She slips inside, pulls thc lock down hard, then tests the handle just to be sure.

Safe.

The taps go on, left to run. She drops the toilet lid and sinks down onto it, elbows to knees, hands clasped. The day — though only just past noon — has already stretched her thin.

The cops. Ozella's relentless calls. The things she'd done to try to cut this off at the root.

Gregor figuring it all out.

Letting his conscience get in the way.

Fuck, fuck, fuck.

What could possibly come next?

Her foot taps against the floor. She nibbles at a nail. Thinking. Running through the options, trying to work out her next move.

Then—

A familiar ping from her back pocket.

Her phone.

She expects Ozella.

But it isn't.

It's an email.

And as soon as she sees the subject line, she has to open it.

14

Gregor is fighting to catch his breath.

From the moment Jessica left, the wheezing started.

It takes him back — back to when he was a dumpy kid in Poland with asthma, back when he'd push himself too hard playing with his mates because that's what you did. Because he didn't know his limits.

Because back then, there were no limits.

A do first and apologise later sort of mentality. A quick puff on the inhaler and he'd be off again.

Now? Now, all there was were limits.

It feels like a block of cement is crushing his chest.

And he didn't need an inhaler. He needed the damn ventilator.

His lips part, a whisper of a sound barely forming. The door is shut, swallowing any chance of being heard. His arms, useless at his sides, can't press the emergency button.

Harder.

Harder.

Each breath is a battle.

And Arek is watching.

Gregor's gaze flicks to the far corner of the room, where those coal-black eyes bore into him. Silent. Unmoving.

He forces himself to stay calm, to take slow, measured breaths.

She'll be back soon.

She'll be back soon.

Just hold on.

And then, finally—

Jessica.

Through the glass pane of the door, he sees her pass by, her silhouette slipping into view. Up until now, every time she left, she always looked in. Always caught his eye with a small, reassuring smile.

Not this time.

Not this morning when she rushed out.

Not now.

A groan escapes his throat as she re-enters the room. It's all he can manage.

He watches, helpless, as she quietly shuts the door behind her.

Then—

She closes the blinds.

"I . . . need,"

The words don't come. They're trapped somewhere deep inside him, shackled in a diaphragm that no longer obeys.

The wheezing is louder now, a broken, stuttering whistle of air.

Is this what drowning feels like?

But where Jessica had rushed to his aid in the past — pressing the call button, summoning nurses, demanding oxygen — now, she just sits.

Watching.

Waiting.

Why isn't she getting help?

She moves to the usual side of his bed. Settles into the chair. Looks him dead in the eyes. The hesitation that had creased her face earlier has vanished, replaced by something colder.

She reaches for his hand, clasping it between hers — not that he can feel it. He has to remember what her touch feels like. Cool, soft, warm beneath his palm.

"Jess," he croaks, barely above a whisper.

She gives a small shake of her head. No hesitation. No faltering. Gregor hears her swallow, as if steeling herself for what she's about to say.

"What kind of life would we have, Greg?"

And just like that, the truth sinks in.

This isn't a question. Not really.

She already knows the answer.

And so does he.

"Please," he rasps between wheezing breaths. "I... need..."

Jessica exhales slowly, bracing herself. "I could've made peace with not having children. I *could* have, Greg. I really think I could." She pauses. Regroups. "It would've eaten at me. Every single day. *Every fucking day.* But I would've done it. For us. For *this*."

Her hands slip away from his.

"But I can't let you tell the police."

Gregor's breath falters.

"I know what you did. I know how much it's killing you," Jessica continues, voice unwavering. "But I won't let you take me down with you. Your life might be over. But mine? I still have too much to do. Too much to take care of."

His lungs tighten. His chest heaves.

Someone — anyone — needs to walk through that door now.

But no one does.

"Jessssssss," her name crawls out of his mouth like a hissing snake. On the other side of his bed, across from Jessica, Arek now stands over him.

You did this, Gregor.

You did this.

Jessica reaches for the pillow.

Gregor watches as she grips it in both hands, steady and certain, and presses it over his face.

At first, the only fight he can summon comes from his neck. A desperate jerking, twisting, trying to claw out the smallest pocket of air.

But it's no use.

Desperation fades to hopelessness.

And as the world darkens, Gregor knows—

He's never waking up from this.

Jessica slowly pulls open the door to Room 201 and peeks into the corridor.

The reception desk beeps rhythmically. The ICU waiting room is busy — coughing, spluttering, murmuring voices mixing with the occasional rattle of a trolley. Further down the corridor, no one lurks.

She's in the clear. Just as she had been out on that rusty old bridge overlooking Deptford Creek.

Jessica pushes the door fully open, letting it rest against the black doorstop. Open. Inviting. Then, with careful precision, she turns the blinds back to open and faces her dead husband.

His eyes are closed now.

Peaceful.

But that, in itself, is wrong.

Gregor didn't sleep peacefully.

Gregor talked just as much in his sleep as he did when he was lucid. Chuntering and muttering, sometimes outright arguing, with people who only existed in his head.

Jessica thinks of all those nights in the Lewisham flat, when she'd stayed up late, only to hear him murmuring through his dreams. She remembers the first time — how she'd woken in the pitch black to the sound of his voice. At first, she'd thought he was on the phone, but when she turned to look, he was flat on his back, deep in sleep.

Instead of being annoyed, she'd lain there, listening. Fascinated.

Over the years, all sorts of names had surfaced from his unconscious ramblings. But one had cropped up more than most.

Arek.

It had come up again this week.

She'd asked. He'd brushed it off. An old school friend, he'd said.

Now, watching Gregor's still body, she almost expects him to start muttering again.

But this time is different.

Jessica swallows hard. It has been nearly two decades since she last took a life. Killing Alfred Mongon, the bastard who had tried to groom her, as she escaped Aston Orphanage had been both satisfying and bloody.

She'd nearly done it again once. Come so close.

But she never thought Gregor would join the same list as Alfred Mongon.

Gregor.

The man who had saved her from herself all those years ago.

"What life would we have?" she'd asked only a matter of minutes earlier.

Somewhere deep inside, Jessica hopes Gregor saw this as mercy. That she was saving him from a life of misery.

She swallows the thought down. Lets the tears fall.

Then she screams.

"Please! Please, somebody help!"

15

A rapid rush of feet.

One . . . two of them at first. Alexandra among them.

A yell for more help in Room 201.

That siren blares. The one that has become so familiar over the last few days.

Three . . . four . . . five.

All moving with that same urgency. The same steely look on their faces.

In the zone.

Their only concern was to save a life that was already over the precipice.

Instructions fly as they buzz around Gregor's body, disturbing the deep eternal peace he is now in.

Determined to bring him back

Extend his misery.

Jessica stands back and lets it unfold.

The compressions begin.

Then the paddles come out.

"Charged . . . clear!" One of those nurses says.

They still believe.

Have to believe.

More compressions.

More shocks.

As the time ticks, their determination and steel erodes.

Jessica sees it. First on Alexandra's face as she is replaced on compressions. The slow shake of the head.

The acceptance of it.

It exchanges like a virus, infecting the others.

After a few minutes, it is over.

And Gregor is finally pronounced dead.

16

It was happening again.

It'd been a while, but she was familiar with the signs.

The shortness of breath. The uncontrollable tremor in her hands. The deep, clawing chill running through her body.

Find a safe space. Rule number one.

Alexandra peels herself away from the bustling ward, away from the concerned glances and well-meaning gestures, and slips into a vacant patient toilet. She doesn't think about that — doesn't care. She just twists the lock, slides down onto the floor, pulls her knees to her chest, and clings on tight, her nails digging into the fabric of her uniform.

Focus on the breathing.

Deep and slow. Count to four. *Inhale for four, hold for four, exhale for four*. Repeat.

Mississippily, she counts in her head, just as her mum had taught her back when these attacks first started in secondary school.

It takes a few minutes, but eventually, it begins to wane. The dizziness fades. The weight in her chest eases.

Alexandra stays there, sitting on the cold tiles.

She's not ready to go back out into the fire just yet.

She can't take another dose of *Are you okay?* Or You should take a break or the inevitable tilt of the head, the sympathetic touch on her arm. She knows they mean well — of course they do. She works with some of the best people she could ever ask for. But today, it's suffocating.

Everyone on shift this morning knew who Jamie had been to her.

But only Nia Edwards, her bestie who'd stuck to her side like glue right through those years of training at Warwick Medical School, knew what Jamie *really* meant.

Their relationship — whatever it was — had been unspoken, unacquainted. A rotten case of *what could have been* if they had met sooner, if things had been mapped out differently by God.

Nia wasn't on shift today, but that didn't matter. Nia was always on the pulse — her words. A terrible pun, considering their line of work.

Alexandra had already seen the text.

She knew exactly how it had come about—one of the nurses had likely mentioned Jamie over lunch, and Nia had gone straight to her phone.

But Alexandra couldn't summon the strength to reply.

Not yet.

Instead, she had poured every ounce of energy into a convincing smile, waving away concerns with a nod, insisting she was fine.

She *had* to be.

There were still people that needed help. There were still lives that could be saved. That was her duty as a critical care nurse. What all her training had been for. So she could make a difference when someone truly needed it.

But then Gregor had died a couple of hours later.

And now, everything felt like it was falling apart.

She hadn't known Gregor long — only a few days — but she'd liked him. There was something about him that put her at ease. He was a good man. Just like Jamie. Alexandra could tell.

But unlike Jamie, Gregor had a shot at life., albeit under a completely new spread of rules and restrictions.

Jamie had never really stood a chance.

His head injury from the crash had been catastrophic. The bleed on his brain had been so severe that the doctors had induced a deep coma the moment emergency surgery was complete.

Alexandra had asked about his chances.

The lead doctor's silence said it all.

So, in the quieter moments on shift, she drank him in.

A battered and bruised shell of the man she'd known.

It was that or nothing.

That first night, Alexandra had kept her distance, watching from afar as Jamie's wife, Jenny, sat at his bedside.

Jenny — who Alexandra liked very much, which only made it worse.

Jenny had held Jamie's hand, played with his fingers, talked about their little boy, Lucas, about some issue at work — banal stuff, desperate to hold on to normal.

She had laughed. She had cried.

Lost in a brutal forest of emotions that Alexandra understood all too well — but only within the confines of her own head.

And when Alexandra prayed, she prayed for Jamie.

Harder than she had ever prayed before.

It didn't change a thing.

Alexandra never swore but it made her want to swear like

she'd never before. And even with her knowledge of Jamie's set reality and the time she had to prepare herself, it didn't make the actual moment his heart beat its last beat any easier to reconcile with.

She had wanted to collapse, right there in the corridor, when the doctor confirmed the time of death and Jenny began to wail.

But Alexandra couldn't.

Not in front of Jenny.

That would have been selfish.

With Gregor, though . . .

It was different.

Yes, he was in a mess. Yes, the crash had left him with irreparable injuries that meant his life would never be the same.

Unlike Jamie, Gregor had been given a second chance. He had a future — one that would take work, adjustment, resilience — but a *future* nonetheless.

And yet, somehow, he was gone too.

That was why this one hurt.

This wasn't supposed to happen.

Alexandra felt like she had failed him.

Like she had been too consumed by her grief for Jamie to see what was happening right in front of her.

She and the other nurses were acutely aware of the issues he'd had with his breathing, that he'd needed constant monitoring.

They had taken for granted that his wife — Jessica, whom Alexandra had never particularly liked — was always by his side.

And just like that, in the briefest of moments, when she had stepped away to use the bathroom, Jessica had come back to find her husband dead.

Another innocent life lost to that awful crash on the M25.

But as Alexandra sits in that bathroom, clutching her uniform with white-knuckled fists, she can't shake the thought.

That maybe — just maybe — her role in all of this had been just as fatal as the crash.

Once she'd finally composed herself, Alexandra left the toilet.

The heat of the ward had faded, replaced by a cold and hushed silence.

Everyone felt it. The glumness. The weight of loss that never truly left, just settled in the walls like old cobwebs, lingering one step behind Death. Over the last four days, it had swept through the ICU, taking twelve victims and leaving this hollow stillness behind, like a calling card.

Speaking of cobwebs — Alexandra noticed a cleaner leaving Gregor's room, a black bag in hand. She wasn't someone Alexandra recognised. Small, with a sharp bob that framed her tight, unreadable eyes, her standard-issue face mask buried the rest of her expression. The cleaner made eye contact. Was there a smile hiding beneath that mask? Impossible to tell.

Alexandra walks towards reception, stopping at Gregor's room.

Now empty. Scrubbed clean.

Jessica was nowhere to be seen — likely taken to one of the family waiting rooms.

The space Gregor had occupied for days was already prepared for someone new.

Like he'd never been there at all.

The worst day of her life was over.

That's how it felt.

Alexandra thinks of her favourite Pixar film, *Inside Out* — of the core memories shaped by Joy, Sadness, Fear, Disgust, and Anger. Memories that shape our messy lives and complex personality. Stay with us forever.

Today feels like one of those. A memory she'll carry for the rest of her life.

She'd stuck it out to the bitter end, despite being given the chance to leave early.

Barbara Wiseman was the charge nurse on duty. Usually, Barbara was a woman of few words, someone who led by what she did rather than what she said. She was a hard nut that was difficult to gauge. She spoke to you if she needed something. Didn't have time for idle chit-chat or gossip. From the very first day Alexandra joined the critical care team, she'd done her best to keep a distance between her and Barbara and only engage her when she needed to.

But today had changed her, too.

Barbara had asked again. Are you sure? She'd said it was understandable. That she'd find cover if Alexandra needed to step away.

But stepping away had never been an option. She couldn't. She had to see the day through.

Just before turning back to work, Barbara placed a hand on Alexandra's shoulder. Her voice was quiet. "Come find me if you need a minute. If you need to talk."

Death has a way of softening even the hardest of nuts.

And so Alexandra soldiered on. Doing what needed to be done. Attending to those who needed her. The entire shift spent behind a protective, masked smile — one that wasn't for her, but for everyone else.

That smile stayed in place right until she was in the changing room.

Head in her locker. Hidden away as the mask dropped.

Behind her, hushed chatter. The crossover of shifts. Those finishing for the day, those starting the late shift, getting caught up with events like it was gossip ripped from Hello! Magazine.

No one pried. No one dragged her into the conversation.

A hand touches her back lightly.

"Night, Alex. I'm... I'm sorry."

Carly Burrow's quiet voice.

"Yeah. Nigh, Carls." She can't stop the sniffle.

The hand slips away and Alexandra is left alone.

And only then do the tears finally escape.

17

She pulls on her coat and grabs the straps of her handbag with both hands.

Only a hundred yards or so separate her from the changing rooms to the exit.

Tomorrow, she's off shift. At least for a few days — unless she gets the call for overtime. Normally, she struggles to say no, afraid of disappointing someone, of giving the wrong impression.

But this time, she'll say no.

Tomorrow, she doesn't plan on leaving the house. She's going to untangle the knots inside her. Maybe call her mum — always a voice of reason when life hands you a rotten apple instead of a juicy one. Again, as she always said.

She steps out of the changing rooms and turns right.

At the end of the corridor, the double doors to reception gleam under the LED lights, the freshly mopped floor shimmering beneath them.

Two policemen stand just inside, flanking a man with his hood pulled up over his head. His hands are cuffed — bloody, dirty. Alexandra always wonders about the stories hidden under those hoods. How people end up in those situations.

She breezes past them.

The exit grows closer.

Fifty yards. Forty. Thirty. Her flats tap a steady, hurried rhythm against the floor.

Then, suddenly—

An old woman bustles through the door, suitcase in tow, stopping Alexandra in her tracks.

At first, Alexandra barely registers the woman.

Just another visitor. Another worried relative.

She walked right past — until she heard the name.

"Gregor. I'm looking for my son, Gregor. He's here. Can you tell me where my son is?"

The voice was sharp, edged with authority, the accent foreign but precise.

Alexandra turns.

She sees this woman, with shoulder-length bleached hair, upright posture, has cornered Devon Newman, one of the new student nurses. He looks frozen, completely caught off guard, his nervousness stitched into the hesitant way he glances around for help.

Alexandra felt duty kick in again.

She approached slowly, careful not to startle the woman.

"Sorry, I couldn't help but overhear. You're looking for Gregor."

"Yes. Where is he?"

Blunt. Direct. No patience for pleasantries.

Alexandra exhaled softly. "Let me take you to the family room. We can talk there."

"I don't want to go to no family room. I want to see Gregor. My son."

Her voice cut through the air, drawing attention. Conversations around them dulled. Drama had a way of pulling people in.

"Please," Alexandra urges, lowering her voice. "Let's talk somewhere private first. Then, I promise, I'll take you to him."

Gregor's mother huffed, shook her head. But after a beat, she relented.

"Well," she says sharply, "you'd better lead the way then."

"We'll go here," Alexandra says quietly.

Gregor's mother — stiff, impatient — nods with forced acceptance. Her face is a picture of someone inconvenienced.

One also totally unaware of the reality.

There's a young couple already in the family room, huddled together, each cradling a paper cup from the hot drinks vendor in their palms. Alexandra recognises them. The boy's mother was brought in during the early hours after a seizure. They've been here ever since — eighteen hours and counting — and it shows in their drained, despondent expressions.

They glance up briefly, taking in the newcomers. Alexandra offers a sympathetic smile. It isn't returned. Their gazes drop back to the floor.

It feels like an intrusion.

Alexandra hesitates. "Let's try one of the other rooms."

"What now?" Gregor's mother snaps, irritation flashing in her dark eyes.

"We should find somewhere more private."

"No, no." She pushes past Alexandra, drops her bag, and squares her shoulders. "I'm not being dragged from room to room. I've had a long flight, and I just want you to tell me where my son is."

A scene is the last thing Alexandra wants. The couple must feel the same — they murmur to each other, then quietly slip out, leaving the space to them.

Alexandra exhales and shuts the door.

"Well?" Ozella's voice is sharp. Urgent.

So Alexandra tells her.

At first, Ozella doesn't cry.

Her mouth slackens, eyes narrowing, deep wrinkles pinching together as she processes Alexandra's words. It's like she's trying to absorb them, trying to rearrange them into something more acceptable.

She had stormed onto the ward with fire in her step, determined to see her son.

Now, Alexandra watches as that fire is extinguished.

Ozella lowers herself into a chair, elbows on her knees, staring at the floor.

"I need a moment," she murmurs.

"Is there anything I can do? I can go and—"

"I said I need a moment."

Alexandra didn't need to be told again.

"I'll be just outside. I'm sorry."

She left.

As she waited, she heard nothing.

Then a few sniffles.

And then, finally, the grief comes pouring out.

EPILOGUE

JESSICA

It was late when I got back from the Spire London East Hospital that night.

Just gone 10.

The rain that had threatened all day had finally checked in, light and fine, bleak and relentless. The kind that soaked through your coat, clung to your skin, made you feel it in your bones.

The first thing I noticed when I stepped inside our flat — it'll never be anything else — was the cold. The heating had been on the fritz again, letting the late autumn chill make itself at home.

But there was something else.

The space, once full of love, laughter, and dreams, now felt occupied by something else entirely. Loneliness' ghost.

Some may say that presence is what I deserve. My penance.

Reading this, reading what really happened to Gregor, you might think my decision was easy. That it was simple. Selfish.

It was anything but.

It's impossible to ignore the fact that Gregor had once saved my life.

All those years ago, when I first came to London, drowning in grief after a brutal miscarriage, trying to drink myself into oblivion. He found me — literally picked me up off the alley floor after one too many kamikaze shots.

He showed me that life might be worth another go.

He became someone I wanted to be better for.

I'd always wanted kids. That much must be clear to you now. I'd already lost one, but I still believed it would happen for Gregor and me. Someday.

Things between us had never been difficult — until our wedding day.

That's when I found out kids were never going to be on the cards.

Not in some abstract, "maybe someday" kind of way. No. They simply weren't in his plans.

And I didn't get a say.

We'd talked about it before. Of course we had. But he always danced around the subject, never committing one way or the other

I'd always figured he'd come around to the idea with time.

He was never so emphatic like Ozella was.

But that confirmation — that finality — was a bitter pill to swallow. One I convinced myself I could live with, given enough time to let it dissolve.

And then the crash happened.

A single minute of carnage.

Twelve dead. Countless lives ruined.

It's hard to explain what I went through. I felt numb. Detached. But the more I toiled over our new reality, the clearer it became: I couldn't see a future for Gregor and me.

Not a happy one, anyway.

Only one filled with resentment. And limitation.

So if you think me heartless for showing him mercy — for freeing us both — then fine. I'll take it like a slap in the face and move on.

But ask yourself this, honestly —

Could you sit across from that person on your sofa, knowing what they'd cost you?

Could you dedicate your life to being their full-time carer?

Could you give up everything you dreamed of — for their mistake?

There was, however, one other thing that truly made my mind up.

The email

It arrived while I was drowning in doubt, mulling everything over, feeling lost and overwhelmed.

And then, like a beacon in the dark, it carved out a new path for me.

I don't mind sharing it with you.

This is how it read:

Subject: St Andrew's Academy Application Update

Dear Mrs. Jessica Johnson,

Thank you for your application for the vacant position at St Andrew's Academy. We are pleased to inform you that you have been selected for a first-stage interview to further discuss your application with our Head Teacher, Mr. Williams.

Interview slots are available for scheduling next week, and you can view and confirm your preferred date and time by following this link.

Please make sure to select a time that aligns with your availability. Once you've confirmed your interview slot, we will send you a confirmation email with further details about the interview process and location.

We look forward to meeting with you and learning more about your qualifications and experiences. If you have any questions or require any additional information before the interview, please do not hesitate to reach out to us.

Thank you for considering a career with St Andrew's Academy. We appreciate your interest in our institution and the potential contributions you may bring to our team.

Best regards,

Patty Maxwell

Officer Administrator

St Andrew's Academy

Yes, I applied for the role.

It was impulsive.

I'd been looking at it again a couple of nights ago while Gregor slept, while I couldn't.

Thinking. Wondering. What if?

I spent an hour filling in the application. Everything I felt, everything I wanted, poured out of me and into the Notes app on my phone. My cover letter practically wrote itself — no bullshit, just me.

I filled in the details, pasted my hastily typed essay, attached a slightly outdated CV from a previous application, and hit send.

And, being honest, I'd not really thought about what would come next.

I didn't have time to.

But then, as I sat in that hospital toilet, contemplating everything, Patty's email landed.

Like a sign.

And suddenly, *I knew*.

Clarity hit me with a rush of emotion so intense it felt like lightning in my veins.

I had purpose again. A future.

And I knew, without a shadow of a doubt, that I couldn't pursue this journey with Gregor by my side.

To me, what I did was the humane solution.

What I did — it freed us both.

I hadn't confirmed my attendance for the interview right away.

I saved it for this moment — settled into my spot on the sofa, wine across from me on the table, heaters humming, filling the space with a warmth that softened the edges of the evening. The sweet scent of pink pepper and pomegranate drifted from the candle perched on the corner of the small bookcase we'd bought last year.

I clicked *Confirm*.

The response landed within seconds. Interview slot booked.

And with it, a second rush of energy.

After four days of living among trauma and death, I finally felt *alive*.

I celebrated by necking the last puddle of wine that filled the bottom of my glass — Sauvignon red — and turned the evening news on.

The crash, once the top story, had begun its slow descent down the news agenda. Now, it was just a nib. A brief mention. A flicker on the screen. If your attention wavered for even a second, you'd miss it.

The female newsreader confirmed that a twelfth person involved in the crash on the M25 last week had died. A male. In his 30s. They didn't share a name.

I'd said my final goodbyes at the hospital. I knew there was no chance Ozella would leave him here. She'd take him back to Poland, back to St. Michael's, to be buried alongside the rest of his family.

And I knew I wouldn't be welcome.

That was that.

I left the news on, letting the chatter fill the silence.

From underneath the sofa, I pulled my laptop out and clicked straight through to Instagram.

I tapped in E.

Clicked straight through to *her* profile.

I had some catching up to do.

ACKNOWLEDGEMENTS

Writing this novella was so much easier than writing When Karma Comes Calling.

Obviously there were much fewer words to write — that's a pretty big factor — but from my perspective, I also benefitted from having the experience of writing When Karma Comes Calling. I learned what ticks for me and I believe I'm starting to find my voice as a writer, too.

This novella is one of three in the complete collection and when I set out to write it, I knew I wanted to explore two areas: different characters that didn't get much air time in the main novel and a different theme or idea that really resonated with me.

I don't know about you, reader, but there are fewer things that grind my gears than seeing someone texting behind the wheel. For this story, I took that and blew it up to make the story that you've just read.

Before writing, I did some research into this issue of texting behind the wheel. I found that a whopping 11 million people in the UK have admitted to using their mobile phone at some point whilst behind the wheel. Less surprising was that phones are the biggest distractions for people while driving and lead to around 2,500 accidents each year.

While a piece of fiction, this novella covered these themes and the life-changing impact a quick look at a text while behind the wheel can have on a person and a family's life.

I promise I'm not going to preach any more... please just don't text while driving. It's not worth it.

Ok, let's use this page for what it is *actually* for.

I dedicated this story to my mum. I was blessed to grow up in a house where I got the best of both worlds. I had a dad that kept me grounded and could be quite tough, while I had a mum that was admittedly soft, but pushed and encouraged me. Growing up, she made me believe I could do and achieve anything I set out to. By no stretch of the imagination am I a best-seller, but I am doing something a lot of people only talk about doing. I thank you, mum, for always encouraging me to follow my passions and to throw myself into things I love.

Big thank you, as always, to my wider family. You guys have been invested in my writing since I started and a lot of you were early readers of this story — even before When Karma Comes Calling made its way out into the world. Your kind words mean everything.

To Christian Storm, who has again designed a wicked cover. His work has had a lot of praise since we started working together, and I'm glad we could keep this collaboration going. I think I tell a half decent story but, boy, do your designs help bring it to life and make everything so much better. You rock!

To my wife and first reader. Thank you for unwavering support and for giving me the time to work on my passion projects. Whether the fact you get to spend that free time watching One Tree Hill is a good thing, I'll let others make that judgement. T.T.A.

To Lewie and your soon to be arriving little brother. You are both my biggest inspiration. I hope you grow up to be proud of these stories.

And lastly to you, the reader. If you have made it this far, thank you — doubly so if you have followed me to this story after finishing When Karma Comes Calling. A writer is nothing without their readers and it is genuinely a heart-warming experience to see my stories out in the world and being read. I only hope you enjoy reading them as much as I do writing them.

Until next time.

ABOUT THE AUTHOR

Tom Bestwick is an East-Midlands-based writer, who has spent his career up to now working in public relations. When Karma Comes Calling was his first novel and will be accompanied by three novellas: The Crash, Black And Blue, and Keep On Digging.

TOMBESTWICKAUTHOR.COM

Printed in Dunstable, United Kingdom

70710401R00075